NURSE AT PINEWOOD

During the eight months she had been a Sister at Pinewood Clinic, Lydia Redmond had never really been satisfied with her relationship with Dr Charles Powell. When she discovered that Charles was a compulsive flirt, she decided to end their friendship, and found romance elsewhere. When a fateful twist in her destiny brought yet another man into her life, he made a great impact and the road to complete happiness seemed wide open for her...

Da **oks**
Long   shire,
d.

British Library Cataloguing in Publication Data.

Cleve, Janita
    Nurse at Pinewood.

    A catalogue record of this book is
    available from the British Library

    ISBN   1-84137-004-5 pbk

First published in Great Britain by Robert Hale & Company, 1972

Copyright © 1972 by Janita Cleve

Cover illustration © Hancock by arrangement with P.W.A.
International Ltd.

Published in Large Print 2000 by arrangement with Robert Hale Ltd.

Dales Large Print is an imprint of Library Magna Books Ltd.

Printed and bound in Great Britain by
T.J. (International) Ltd., Cornwall, PL28 8RW

Chapter One

Pinewood, the large Clinic set in isolation among the pine trees of a large wood in North Norfolk, was silent and sleeping as Sister Lydia Redmond made her way along its rambling corridors on night duty. Rain was beating at the tall windows, and the wind howled angrily outside, seeking any chink or gap to gain noisy entry. It was October and it didn't seem possible to Lydia that the summer had flown like a migrating bird.

Her tall figure fled in shadow before her as she passed under a lamp, and she drew a sharp breath as she considered the long hours of the night still before her. She had been at Pinewood for eight months now, and in that time she still hadn't discovered if she were in love with Charles Powell, one of the doctors. He had quite a reputation with the nurses and the girls in the nearby village, but he had professed love for Lydia almost from the first moment they had met, and he had almost succeeded in sweeping her off her feet.

She sighed as she went on, intent upon checking the small operating theatre, and her mind was slipping away from her normal thoughts of duty as she pushed open the swing doors that led into the theatre. Her rubber soled shoes made no sound on the tiled floor, and she frowned slowly when she saw a light had been left on at the far end of the theatre, near the small anteroom where they scrubbed before an operation. She tightened her grip on her torch as she walked noiselessly across to the light switch, and she was about to plunge the theatre into darkness when she heard a sharp, suppressed giggle coming from the anteroom.

Lydia froze instantly, and her pulses raced. Then she heard a man's voice, low and insistent, and her blood seemed to run cold as she recognized it as Charles Powell's.

'Come on, Diana, give me another kiss!'

Lydia backed away almost without thought, her mind blank with shock, and she turned and departed as noiselessly as she had entered the theatre. Once in the corridor she paused and took a deep breath, her mind reeling, her balance affected by her shock. She put a wavering hand against the wall and rested her weight against it. There had been rumours that Charles was seeing Diana Dillon, the new nurse, on the side, but Lydia had discounted the rumours with the contempt they deserved. But now the few words she had overheard were ringing in her ears like some painful knell of doom.

Charles was in the dark anteroom with Nurse Dillon, and there was no need for Lydia to wonder what was going on!

Lydia closed her eyes and swayed slightly. It was her duty to confront them and warn Nurse Dillon that she was breaking strict regulations! But Lydia knew she could never find the nerve to do her duty in that respect. She pictured Charles' handsome face, and knew fleeting despair. She would never love him now! But she was also conscious of a small measure of relief flaring up inside her shocked mind. She hadn't fallen in love with him in the eight months they had been seeing one another. She liked him immensely, but liking, although akin to loving, was not the same, and she heaved a long sigh as she tried to overcome her shock and substitute calmness for her trembling realization.

But she could not leave matters as they were, and she steeled herself and pushed open the swing door again, peering into the theatre and calling loudly.

'Nurse Dillon, are you there?' She made no effort to enter, and there was a lump in her throat as she awaited reaction to her voice.

'Yes, Sister?' There was a note of panic in the girl's voice, and the next instant she appeared from the anteroom, looking rather panic stricken as she switched out the light and came quickly to where Lydia was standing. 'I was just checking that everything was all right in here,' Nurse Dillon went on edgily.

'Well it's time you went for your night meal,' Lydia said, ignoring the fact that Charles Powell was standing in the darkness in the anteroom. 'You'd better get away now, while everywhere is quiet.' She looked at her watch and nodded. 'I'll go to the dining room as soon as you come back.'

'Very well, Sister!' Diane Dillon was a tall slim blonde with bright blue eyes, and in the month that she'd worked on nights with Lydia she had shown her worth. She was most able as a nurse, but she had a failing in that she could not help flirting with the male staff. Even the porters had come under her spell, and Lydia had no doubt that Charles had found her captivating.

Lydia walked along the corridor for a short way with the girl, pausing when they reached the stairs that led down to the lower floors.

'Report to my office when you return from your meal,' Lydia said softly. 'Then I'll get away for mine.'

'Very good, Sister!' The girl threw her a speculative glance, then descended the stairs quickly, but Lydia stood waiting until she had gone before she turned swiftly to return to the theatre.

She didn't expect to find Charles still in the anteroom. He would have fled along the corridor in the opposite direction the moment she left. But she had to check, and she switched on all the lights in the theatre before looking around, finding it as she expected, silent and deserted. She stood in the centre of the anteroom and looked around slowly, her mind hearing again the intense words that Charles had spoken. And he was the man who was supposed to be in love with her!

A thin, cynical smile touched her lips and she shook her head as she recalled some of the times they'd spent together, when he had spoken of his undying love for her. But she had long suspected that he liked a different face at times, and she guessed now that all the rumours of the past months had been true.

But where did it leave her? Lydia switched out the lights again and departed, firming her lips. She knew instinctively that she had never been in love with Charles, and yet there was something about him that attracted her. He was a cheerful man, with an engaging smile, and she had been lonely during her first months at Pinewood.

She went back to the office on the ground floor near the main entrance, and had hardly sat down at the desk when a soft footstep outside caused her to look up quickly. She saw Dr Tim Fairfax step into the doorway, and she smiled instantly

'Good evening, Doctor,' she greeted. 'I've just had a look at Mrs Fulmar and she seems to be more comfortable. Do you want to see her now?'

'I've just looked into her room,' he said. 'Is

there anything else that requires my attention now?'

'Nothing, Doctor.' Lydia looked into his blue eyes and found them studying her critically. She liked Tim Fairfax, the other resident doctor, and she had often wished that Charles Powell had been as quiet and sincere. But men were not saints, and she knew she had to accept Charles as he was if she wanted to find a future with him.

She dragged her mind back from Charles and concentrated upon the tall, good looking man before her. He never seemed to be off duty, and Lydia guessed that he took over much of Charles Powell's duties. That was one of the reasons why Charles could get around so much. Lydia thought it strange that there were never any rumours circulating about Tim Fairfax, but all the nurses respected him, and talked about him with admiration when they had anything at all to say. She found herself beginning to wonder about his life. He had been here at the Clinic for about five years, she knew, and wondered what made him tick. Where did he find his pleasures? Why didn't he get out and about like Charles Powell? He was only about thirty, a year or two younger than Charles, and yet the two men were poles apart, and never seemed to be on friendly terms.

'Something wrong, Sister?' Fairfax demanded, jolting Lydia from her thoughts, and she blinked as she dragged her mind back to the present.

'Wrong, Doctor?' she queried.

'You're staring at me? Have I got lipstick on my cheek, or something?'

Lydia laughed musically. 'That would be the day, wouldn't it?' she demanded, and felt a queer tugging sensation in her breast as she imagined what must have been happening in the anteroom when she overheard Charles talking to Nurse Dillon.

'Why do you say that?' He came nearer to the desk, then sat down on the chair beside it, leaning forward and staring at her as if expecting a firm answer.

'Well, you don't seem the kind of man who would do anything like that on duty, Doctor,' she ventured.

'You think that I'm above being human?'

'I didn't say that! But I imagine you wouldn't mix business with pleasure.'

He smiled, and Lydia relaxed a little as he leaned back in his seat and glanced around the office.

'How long have you been with us now, Sister?' It was an unexpected question, and Lydia frowned as she replied.

'I came here at the beginning of March, Doctor. It's almost eight months now.'

'Time passes quickly, doesn't it? Do you like it here?'

'Very much!' Lydia wondered why he was talking to her like this. He had never been anything but formal before. They had talked often enough about their patients, but he rarely spoke so generally, and she had been under the impression for a very long time that he was innately shy.

'What made you bury yourself in a remote

spot like this?' he continued.

'I'm not exactly buried here,' she retorted, sitting up a little straighter in her seat.

'Of course you get out quite a lot with Charles Powell.' A strange note attached itself to his voice as he spoke, and Lydia studied his intent face. His blue eyes were very sharp and bright, and she felt a pang stab through her as he looked at her. There was something about his gaze that had always disturbed her when she felt it upon her, and now she mentally squirmed as she tried to stare him out. He smiled slowly, and she noticed how white his teeth were.

'Not any more,' she said firmly, almost before she realized what she was saying.

'What do you mean?' He was leaning forward again, holding her gaze almost against her will.

'I shouldn't have said that aloud,' she floundered, moistening her lips.

'All right, I didn't hear you,' he said instantly, but his pale eyes narrowed and he seemed to be peering straight through her exterior, as if he could read what was in her mind and her thoughts.

'You shouldn't stare at a poor girl like that, Doctor,' she said desperately.

'Really, Sister?' His tones suggested surprise at her words, but she had the feeling that he was not surprised. 'That's a strange statement, coming from you.'

'I'm sorry!' Lydia shook her head. 'I must be overtired tonight! I really don't know what I'm saying. I'm getting into deep water, aren't I?'

He smiled briefly. 'Where is your home?' he asked.

'London!'

'You go there about once a month. Do you visit your parents?'

'Yes! Mother insists that I go home at least once a month. She's afraid of losing touch with me.'

'I imagine you're the kind of girl who wouldn't dream of severing family connections.'

She dearly wanted to ask him questions

about himself, but she could not find the nerve to. She just nodded, and watched his attractive face. He had a small nose and pleasant features, and his mouth was well shaped and full, denoting a generous nature. She knew he was a quiet type, and he never seemed to get flustered or in a panic, no matter what emergency burst upon him.

'You interested me with your words about not going out with Charles Powell again,' he said. 'What do you mean by it?'

Lydia shrugged. 'I'm sorry, Doctor, but I don't wish to discuss my personal affairs.'

'Of course not! I am being nosey, I know, but I wouldn't like to see a girl like you getting into complicated situations with a man like Charles Powell.'

'What exactly do you mean, Doctor?' Lydia was sitting stiffly now, and she moistened her lips as she stared at him.

'It's none of my business, as you so rightly reminded me, He said, smiling thinly. 'I think we'd better change the subject.'

'I don't want to change the subject!' Her tones were sharp.

He looked into her face, and she felt a thrill go through her as she watched his expressive eyes. He was different tonight! The knowledge seeped into her mind, scalding among the thoughts already there. She caught her breath as she suddenly realized that perhaps he had seen Charles in some compromising situation with one of the nurses! But she didn't want to hear about it despite her insistence that they didn't change the subject.

'I'd better go and get some sleep in case you have to call me out,' he said slowly, getting to his feet. 'Goodnight, Sister.' There was a smile on his face and he seemed to tower over her as he paused for a moment in front of the desk.

'Doctor Fairfax!' Her tones were suddenly husky. 'I have the feeling that you want to say something to me!'

He stopped in midstride and turned to look at her. For a moment they were motionless, silent, and Lydia could hear her last words echoing in her mind. He had stiffened as he turned, and seemed to be on the defensive, but there was no expression on his face, and he slowly shook his head.

'Sorry if I gave you that impression,' he retorted at length. 'I was just interested in what you had to say about your future. You see—!' He paused and a grimace touched his face, and then he smiled slowly. 'I was interested in you the moment I saw you here eight months ago, but Charles Powell got to you first or I might have tried to make friends with you. Does that answer your question?'

'Yes, Doctor!' Lydia could hardly believe her ears. She stared at him as if he had suddenly sprouted another head, and he smiled and turned away, departing quickly.

Lydia leaned back in her seat and stared at the doorway, listening to his faintly receding footsteps. She was astonished by what he had said. His words made her think of him in a different light, and she realized that the few minutes he had been talking to her showed him as a totally different character to the one she had supplied him with in the absence of details about him.

She was interrupted by the return of Nurse Dillon, who came into the office furtively, as if she still suspected that Lydia knew what was going on in the anteroom.

'I'm all ready to take over, Sister,' the girl reported, and Lydia got to her feet slowly, still lost in her thoughts.

'I shan't be more than thirty minutes, Nurse,' she responded.

Nurse Dillon moved around the desk to take Lydia's place, and she watched Lydia all the time. Lydia smiled to herself when she noted the other's fears, and she could understand why Charles had dallied with this girl. But he was not stable enough to stay with any one girl, and Lydia was beginning to let her mind accept the fact. She had blinded herself to it for too long, but then she hadn't been in love with Charles herself, so it didn't really matter about all the other girls.

She was most thoughtful as she went along to the dining room, and she helped herself to a meal from the large hotplate. There was no-one else in the dining room, and she sat at a corner table and ate thoughtfully.

She would have to let Charles know that she knew about his moments with Nurse Dillon. That was obvious, and she felt a certain amount of satisfaction at the thought which surprised her, for she detested scenes of any kind. But she was not going to continue in the way they had been living. She wanted nothing more to do with Charles, and he could go blithely along in his own sweet way.

The sound of the door being thrust open jerked her from her thoughts, and she looked up quickly, fearing that Nurse Dillon had come to summon her to some unexpected emergency, but she saw Charles himself entering, and her face flushed as she realized it was he. She watched him as he paused on the threshold, so sure of himself that his manner amounted almost to arrogance. He went to the stove and poured himself a cup of coffee, then came towards her, smiling widely.

'Hello, Sweetheart!' He sat down and set his coffee before himself. 'How's night duty going?'

She looked into his handsome face for a moment, noting that his blue eyes were like Tim Fairfax's, but sharper and colder. He continued to smile, and she suddenly felt revulsion sweep through her mind. She could imagine him holding Nurse Dillon in his arms in that darkened anteroom, and she heard his husky voice once more, talking exactly as he had spoken to her many times in the privacy of his car when they had been out together.

'I'm doing all right,' she responded slowly. 'What about you, Charles?'

'I've spent a quiet evening,' he retorted. 'It's always the same when I can't get near you.'

'You were very quiet in the anteroom up in Theatre,' she said, and saw his pale eyes widen. He sat upright and clenched his hands, and she smiled at the comic expression of incredulity that came to his handsome features.

'What on earth are you talking about, Lydia?' he demanded, and she knew he was going to brazen it out.

She shook her head as she sighed. 'It really isn't any of my business, when you think about it,' she said slowly. 'Except that kissing a girl on duty is against the regulations, and Nurse Dillon is in my charge.'

'She told you about it?' He shook his head in disbelief, knowing it would be useless to deny it in the face of her quiet confidence.

'She didn't have to. I overheard you.' Lydia smiled as she related the incident, and she saw his face flush a little, 'But don't worry about it, Charles,' she went on. 'I'm not going to say anything to Nurse Dillon this time. It's up to you whether you

23

mention it to her. But stay away from the nurses when they're on duty or you'll be in trouble as well as them.'

'I didn't mean any harm,' he said sharply.

'I'm sure you didn't do any harm,' she replied.

'Oh! I didn't think you were that understanding, Lydia!'

'I understand only too well! But I don't understand you, Charles. Why have you been trying to get me serious about you when you couldn't be serious about me to save your life? It's really none of my business that you run after every pretty face you see. There's no understanding between us, is there? So you go right ahead and enjoy yourself. But don't expect me to go out with you ever again.'

He looked into her determined brown eyes and studied her harshly set face. Then he nodded and grinned, and he gulped his coffee quickly.

'All right,' he said thinly. 'If you can't take a joke! I suppose I have been wasting my time with you.'

'That's the only reason why you've remained so interested in me,' she retorted. 'You couldn't add me to your long list of conquests, could you? But I'm sure I'm not your first failure, and you haven't grieved too long after the others, surely! You are not the type. It's been fun knowing you, Charles. I shall miss those trips we used to take, but you've never been certain that I could be the girl you could settle down with, and in eight months I've never come anywhere near to falling in love with you.'

'So it's over!' He shrugged, then got to his feet. 'I don't like scenes, do you?'

'Certainly not!' She smiled at him as she looked up into his blue eyes. 'It's been nice knowing you, Charles.'

'I agree. See you around, Lydia!'

He turned and walked out of the dining room, and she sagged a little in her seat, finding herself faced with a different future to the one she had come to accept. There would be no more exciting evenings with a man who certainly knew how to charm women, but she was not disappointed by the turn of events, only a little shocked at the way the situation had fallen upon her, and its speed. She had always managed to make her own life interesting, being born with a capacity for solitude that suited her present surroundings. And now she wouldn't have to wonder if every little rumour that she heard about Charles was true or not! That would be a relief. Now it was no longer any of her business!

She finished her meal slowly, thoughtfully, and then went back on duty, and her mind was strangely clear and bright considering the events which had taken place. But she felt that the short talk she had with Tim Fairfax had done something to alter her frame of mind. In all the months she had been at Pinewood she had never considered him as human. But now she knew differently, and the revelation had come at a fateful moment. That knowledge did something to her inside. It made her feel as if forces beyond any of their control were at work about them, and although she felt it was ridiculous to accept the thought, she did so nevertheless!

Chapter Two

Going off duty next morning, Lydia was tired and ready for bed, but she found she could not sleep. She had been thoughtful most of the night, and felt strangely affected by the short talk she'd had with Tim Fairfax. The fact that she had discovered Charles Powell's true nature, and had finished with him after eight months of friendship, did not seem to worry her at all, which was most surprising. Now, lying in bed trying to induce slumber to visit her, listening to the rain beating against the window, she tried to clear her mind of all disturbing and conflicting thought.

But impressions kept darting through her mind, and she was aware that there was a thrilling sensation inside her, as if she were expecting something very exciting to happen. It was crazy, she knew, to let her mind get into such a state, and she had never been bothered overmuch before by imagination. She sighed and forced her mind to relax, then closed her eyes and tried to drift into sleep.

Eventually she did sleep, and did not awaken until early afternoon, when she opened her eyes to find a weak sun trying to filter into the room. She arose and went along to take a shower, then dressed before going to the dining room for a meal. She found Diana Dillon in the room, already eating her meal, and Lydia went to join the girl.

'Had a good sleep?' Lydia demanded cheerfully.

'Yes, thank you, Sister.' The girl seemed awkward, and Lydia paused for a moment as she wondered if Charles had said anything to her about the previous evening's incident. The next moment Nurse Dillon broached the subject herself, her face flushing and showing sheepishness. 'Sister, about last night,' she began uneasily.

'Doctor Powell has told you that I know about it?'

'Yes, Sister! Look, nothing really happened. I went into the theatre to check that everything was all right, and Doctor Powell followed me in.'

'That's all right, Nurse. Forget about it, and don't worry. I shall say nothing to anyone else. But remember that when you're on duty that sort of thing must never happen. If anyone else had discovered you then I expect you would have been packing, this morning.'

'Would I have been dismissed?'

'Most certainly! Doctor Powell knows that, too!'

'What I really wanted to say was that I'm sorry it happened because you have been going steady with Doctor Powell. He told me last night that he'd finished with you, Sister. Was it because of what had happened?'

'That finished us, of course,' Lydia said in

even tones. 'But don't upset yourself about it because there was nothing between us. I wasn't in love with Doctor Powell, or anything like that. And you'll discover for yourself, if you start going around with him, that he's incapable of loving and cherishing a girl in the normal way. He's much too selfish and self-centred.'

'I'm so relieved that he means nothing to you. I would have been hurt if I had been the cause of any unhappiness for you.'

Lydia smiled. She shook her head slowly as she began to eat her meal. She couldn't feel sorrow at parting from Charles. He had been good fun, and they'd been friends, but she had never been attracted to him in the slightest, and he must have realized that long before she did. She thought of Tim Fairfax, and a thrill shot along her spine, causing her to catch her breath. She sighed a little as she finished her meal, and then she took her leave and went back to her room. She wanted to go into the nearby village to do some shopping, and she paused as she realized that she wouldn't be able to get a lift from Charles any more.

Lydia checked the weather and decided that the watery sun would remain shining for the rest of the afternoon at least, although there were some ominous clouds far across the sky. The village, a very small and remote place with the imposing name of Thurling St Clements, lay four miles away, and beyond it the larger town of Norton was some eight miles distant. Lydia thought for a moment, not relishing the thought of walking four miles, and she had some necessary shopping to do. There was no bus service, and she shook her head in frustration as she considered the situation. Then she remembered that Nurse Kent had a bicycle, and she went to ask the girl for the loan of the machine.

Nurse Kent was on day duty, and she readily agreed to loan Lydia her bicycle.

'It's in the shed near the greenhouse, Sister,' the girl said. 'You'll find a plastic mackintosh in the saddlebag, and I expect you'll need it before you get back.'

'I think it will keep fine,' Lydia said optimistically.

'Don't leave it too late coming back because there are no lights on the machine,' Nurse Kent went on.

'Thanks, and I'll take good care of it,' Lydia told her.

She departed and went to the shed for the cycle, wheeling it along the drive to the road, and as she reached the main gate where the car park was she saw, with fleeting concern, Nurse Dillon getting into Charles Powell's car. Lydia sighed as she went on, and she saw Charles grinning at her as she mounted the cycle and began to pedal towards the distant village.

There was a fairly strong wind blowing which she hadn't taken into consideration, and being out of practice with a bicycle, Lydia was hard put to maintain fast progress, but eventually she reached a sheltered stretch of the road and was able to speed along in top gear. She wavered a little when Powell passed her very closely in his car, and she did not doubt that he was enjoying the spectacle of her riding a cycle. But she pushed all thoughts of him resolutely out of mind and continued.

She reached the village in a surprisingly short time, and soon did her shopping. There was not much to be done or seen in Thurling St Clements, and she had only just started her trip back to the Clinic when rain began to spatter about her.

Stopping at the side of the road, Lydia took out the plastic mackintosh and put it on, and she continued cheerfully, not minding the least about the weather. But soon the rain was coming down quite hard and she was forced to stop under some trees on a lonely stretch of the road and take shelter. She watched the rain pelting down on the road, and she felt rueful as she thought of the three miles still to be travelled.

The late afternoon was gloomy, and the clouds overhead were hastening the onset of darkness. Lydia knew she had to get back to the Clinic before nightfall, and she began to worry about the situation. Cycling in the rain for three miles would he better than waiting for the rain to stop, only to walk the rest of the way because of darkness! She took a deep breath, considered for a moment or two longer, then pushed the cycle on to the road and started again.

The mackintosh kept a great deal of the rain off her, but her hair was soaked, and rain was dribbling down her face. Her feet and legs were soon drenched, and she pedalled furiously along the deserted road. But she didn't mind in the least that she was getting wet, and treated the whole matter as a joke. She went downhill on a bend, realizing too late that she was travelling too fast for the conditions of the road, and at the sharpest part of the bend the cycle began to wobble. Lydia clutched at the brakes and put the machine into a skid. The next instant the front wheel touched the loose gravel near the verge and promptly twisted sideways. Before Lydia was hardly aware what was happening, the machine had up-ended and she was flying forward over the handlebars.

It was fortunate that there was a grass verge, but all the same Lydia landed heavily upon it, and rolled helplessly until she finished on her back staring up at a large tree whose branches wept copiously upon her. She was breathless and a little shocked, and could not move for a moment, and she could hear the back wheel of the cycle spinning madly. A car screeched nearby and she lifted her head slightly to peer at the road, and she was surprised to see Tim Fairfax getting out of the vehicle to come hurrying towards her.

Lydia began to struggle into a sitting position, but Fairfax reached her and dropped to one knee upon the wet grass.

'Lie still a moment,' he commanded. 'Have you hurt yourself? I was looking for you and had just come around the bend back there when I saw you coming off that infernal machine.'

'I'm all right, I think,' Lydia said shakily. 'No bones broken or other injuries, except a little shock, no doubt. I'm not used to riding a cycle.'

He helped her to her feet and looked at her, a thin smile on his handsome face. Lydia was only too conscious of her wet face and bedraggled hair, and she clutched at his arm as she swayed a little.

'You're not all right,' he said instantly, slipping a supporting arm at her back. 'Come and sit in the car for a moment. Why didn't you let me know you were coming into the village this afternoon? I would have brought you. I did ask for you at the Clinic and learned that you'd cycled in, and on a day like this! You must be out of your head!'

'One has to get shopping done, and there are no buses in this area.' Lydia allowed him to take her to the car, and she sighed with relief as she sat in the front passenger seat and he closed the door on her. She watched him go back for the cycle, and he brought it to the car and put it in the back, standing up against the rear seat. 'You'll ruin your upholstery,' she protested. 'I'm soaking wet as well.'

'I'll put you in the boot,' he retorted with a smile as he got into the car. For a moment he sat looking at her, and again she was only too conscious of the fact that she must look like a drowned animal. 'In future you let me know when you want to leave the Clinic,' he said severely. 'I'll drive you anywhere you want to go.'

'But I couldn't put you to any trouble,' she protested.

'Why not? You let Powell drive you around! What's wrong with me?'

'Nothing!' She shook her head vehemently, and splashed him with drops of water. 'I didn't mean it like that! I'm independent, too, and I don't like asking anyone for anything.'

'I was going to ask you out for the afternoon and evening, but you got away before I could get to you,' he said firmly.

'Now you're soaked and you'll go back to the Clinic and spend the rest of the time drying off to go on duty!'

'I can soon change,' she retorted, and caught her breath. She hadn't meant to say that, and she saw a smile come to his face.

'All right. I'll drive you to the Clinic now and wait for you. I'm not going to take any chances of missing out on you this time. When you first arrived I was too slow, and Powell got to you first. It's not going to happen again.'

He started the car and drove on, and Lydia watched him in some amazement. He glanced at her and smiled.

'You look surprised,' he said cheerfully. 'What's wrong?'

'I'm amazed, Doctor,' she said.

'My name is Tim!' he reminded. 'What amazes you?'

'I always thought you were a woman hater! Your attitude around the Clinic gave me that impression.'

'Because I wouldn't look at any of the

other nurses?' He smiled slowly. 'Why should I have chosen second best? You interested me the first moment I saw you, and I knew Powell well enough to know that sooner or later he would drop you, so I waited for that moment, and here it is.'

Lydia studied him as he drove back to the Clinic, and she liked what she saw. He had always impressed her as being a very handsome man, and the fact that he didn't lead a social life had made her think seriously about him more than once. But she was still surprised by this sudden change in his manner, although it was obvious that her own changes were responsible for his. Yet she had attained a mental picture of him that warned her he was not human in his approach to others. He had shunned all company and kept himself very much to himself. Now here he was acting as extroverted as Charles Powell himself.

When they reached the Clinic he drove up to the side door and parked, turning to her with a smile.

'We can't go far this evening,' he said, 'but I had planned to take you for a long drive. However there will be other times, Lydia, so I'll content myself taking you out for a couple of hours. You'll be going on duty tonight, and I wouldn't want to tire you out.' He smiled as he paused and studied her for a moment. 'I am sorry,' he said slowly. 'I ought to ask you if you'd care to go out with me before I make plans. I took it for granted that you would agree.'

'Why?' she asked.

'I don't know. I just got the feeling that you would.'

'Well I wouldn't want to disappoint you now, so I'll go in and change.'

'What about tea?' he asked. 'Shall we go for a drive after tea?'

'Just as you wish.'

'It will be rather late to get anything out at this time. I could take you to dinner in town later. Does that sound attractive?'

'Very!' Lydia was conscious of the rain

drops seeping down her neck and sending a series of cold shivers along her spine. 'I shall be hard pushed to make myself look presentable again after this drenching, but if you don't mind the new washed-out look then it will be all right.'

'I think you look perfectly beautiful,' he retorted seriously.

She smiled at him and opened the car door.

'I'll put the cycle away for you,' he said. 'You run along in now, and I'll see you out here at the car at six-thirty. Will that be all right?'

She nodded, still smiling, and there was warm regard in her mind for him. She left him and hurried into the building, and a glance at the darkening sky told her that the rain was abating. But she could not be angry at it for the way the afternoon turned out, and she went up to her room to make what repairs she could to her appearance.

She took a hot shower to chase the chill out of her bones, and soon readied herself for the evening. She sat in front of her mirror and studied her face, thinking of Tim and wondering what was developing about her. She was surprised to know that he had taken to her from the first moment of her arrival, and all the time she had been going around with Charles, Tim had been waiting and hoping for the break.

Lydia could not control the strange feelings that came to her with this knowledge. Tim Fairfax had been a secret admirer for months, and now he was not going to miss any opportunity. He had made it abundantly clear that he wouldn't miss out for a second time, and she felt her pulses race as she recalled the powerful intensity of his eyes. Now that she could think about him so, she realized that she had always been subconsciously attracted to him. She had spent a lot of her duty hours at night wondering about him, trying to analyze his remoteness, and she had been on the wrong track from the very start.

When she thought of Charles and Diana

Dillon she could not help wondering why she didn't feel the slightest pang of emotion at their unexpected parting. But now she knew. If Charles had left a gap in her life by his sudden departure from it then Tim had promptly stepped into the place, and he filled it completely.

The more she pondered over that particular area of speculation the more convinced she became that her future prospects were good. But what surprised her was her own natural acceptance of Tim Fairfax in Charles Powell's place. She had never been in love with Charles, and yet Tim seemed to arouse deeper responses from her. She thought of the way her feelings had sharpened when she'd sat in his car with him, and she thought of his face and pictured his lips, feeling a shudder of anticipation touching her nerves as she imagined what it would be like to be kissed by him.

Lydia got to her feet with a sigh and glanced at her watch. She wasn't pleased with the way her hair had gone, but it was all she could do with it. At such short notice it was a wonder she was able to achieve any degree of presentability. She felt shivery as she waited out the last moments before going down to Tim's car, and she wondered why the thought of going out with him should fill her with such joy.

It was raining again when she finally went down to the side door, and she was surprised to find Tim already seated in the car. He opened the door for her as she ran across to him, and she was breathless as she settled in the seat at his side.

'We must be crazy to go out like this,' he remarked, smiling at her.

'We're in the dry now,' she retorted.

'And you're looking very lovely!' His pale eyes sparkled as he watched her. 'This is a great moment for me, Lydia. I've dreamed of it for a very long time, and I'd almost despaired of it ever coming about.'

'Well here I am, so your prayers must have been answered,' Lydia said lightly. 'I would have gone out with you before, if you'd asked me. There was never any understanding between Charles and me.'

'I was tempted a great many times to say something to you.' He started the car and switched on the headlights. 'Where shall we go?'

'I don't mind in the least, so long as you get me back here in time to go on duty.'

'Good. Then leave it to me.'

She nodded and relaxed in her seat, aware that his nearness was causing her mind to sense strange feelings that had not yet arisen from her subconscious. She felt nervous for some unaccountable reason, and there was excitement in her like silver threads woven into a dark piece of cloth.

Tim was rather silent now, and Lydia could not help wondering if he were inherently shy. He might have been desperate enough for her company to push himself this far, and then his courage might have deserted him. She smiled softly as she watched him driving, and in the gloom he did not take his eyes off the road. She didn't find the silence awkward, and made no effort to break it.

But presently he glanced at her and smiled as he caught her eye.

'I've often wondered what you would be like to talk to off duty,' he said. 'Now you're with me I just don't know what to say. Perhaps I'm too aware of the way I pushed myself on to you. What do you think about that?'

'I don't know! What should I think?' she countered. 'If a man wants to get to know a woman then he has to take the initiative. I think you handled it very well.'

'I was pushed by the fact that Powell pipped me the fiirst time, and I thought last night that you might go off out and meet someone else after you broke with Powell.'

'I'm not really like that,' she said. 'I went out with Charles because he was available, but we were only friends. I didn't have any deep feelings for him!'

'I was aware of that or I would have given

up hope a long time ago.' He grinned at her, and she watched his profile as he turned his attention to his driving once more.

Lydia could see the lights of the town shining ahead, and she folded her arms and leaned back in her seat, half wishing that they could have gone on driving forever. It was very comfortable and cosy in the car with the heater working and the rain outside pattering against the windscreen!

'It's still a bit early for a meal,' Tim said. 'Shall we go on driving for a bit, then come back?'

'Just as you wish,' she told him. 'I don't mind so long as we get back to the Clinic in time for duty.'

'You're quite a stickler for duty, but the nurses all have a lot of good to say about you,' he remarked. 'I've listened avidly to everything said about you.'

'I wish I had known about this earlier,' she retorted.

'Does it make you happy to know you've had a secret admirer?' He was smiling.

'It bolsters my ego.' She nodded as she studied him. 'I rather like you, Tim!'

'That's nice to know.' He slowed the car for a moment and looked at her. 'I used to wonder what passed through your mind whenever you looked at me around the Clinic. Tell me about it.'

'What can I say? I thought nothing at the time, but in retrospection, and in view of what has happened since yesterday, I get the impression that I have been intrigued by you.' She paused, shaking her head. 'Am I being too bold, or has your boldness put me into a similar frame of mind?'

'I'm not going to question it,' he said. 'Let's leave that as it is.'

'Why don't you tell me something about yourself?' she asked.

'There's not much to tell. Before I came here I was in a Clinic in Scotland. Let me see, I was there three years! Before that I was at St Martin's Hospital in London.'

'You have a home somewhere, surely!'

'In London – Wimbledon! When we get a

couple of days off I shall take you home with me. Your parents live in London, didn't you say?'

'Shepperton, actually! We've been near neighbours and didn't know it.'

He nodded. 'I feel cosy in your company, Lydia. I hope we are going to spend some time together in future!'

'If you want to!' She was unable to say what her true feelings were at that moment, and she didn't dare question herself too deeply. But she knew she wanted to be in his company more than she had ever wanted to be with Charles Powell. She smiled when she thought of Charles taking out Nurse Dillon. He hadn't been upset at all when she told him she wouldn't see him again. He was that kind of man. Association didn't mean anything to him. He could take a girl or leave her! But she knew Tim was not like that, although she hardly knew him. She sensed what he was like, and she knew her intuition would not let her down.

Later they went back to town and Tim

took her into the largest hotel and they had a meal together. Lydia enjoyed herself immensely. She could not believe that this was the first time they had been out together. He didn't seem like a stranger, no matter how she viewed him, and when she thought of all the times they'd spoken formally to one another on duty she could hardly accept that he was now the same man.

'I suppose I'd better start thinking of getting you back to the Clinic,' he observed at length. They were sipping drinks and listening to soft music being played over a loudspeaker.

Lydia glanced at her watch and nodded instantly. 'If we delay much longer then I shall be late,' she said.

'Come on then. We are about finished here.'

He paid the bill and they departed, and when they got into the car rain began to splash down again. But nothing could detract from Lydia's pleasure, and her brown eyes twinkled as she leaned back in her seat and let her mind revisit the pleasures of the evening.

'Thank you, Lydia,' he said at length when they had turned into the driveway leading up to the Clinic. 'I can't remember the last time I enjoyed myself so much, and that's the truth. I've been waiting a long time for this evening, I can tell you.'

'Thank you, Tim,' she replied. 'I've had a truly wonderful time. It was all the more pleasant because it was so unexpected.'

She saw him smile as he brought the car to a halt at the side door.

'Does that mean you'll be prepared to come with me again?' he asked quietly.

'Any time that you wish to take me out,' she replied.

He switched off his lights and turned to her. Lydia caught her breath when she divined his intention, and as his arms touched her shoulders she closed her eyes. This was quite out of keeping with her true nature, she realized. She had never been a flirt at any time in her life, and she had always been careful of her associations. But this was different, and she went eagerly into Tim Fairfax's arms.

When he did kiss her she felt a wondrous emotion steal through her, and she clenched her hands, resisting the temptation to throw herself into his embrace and give herself up to her strange feelings. She tried to cling to some part of the sanity in her mind, but she knew she was fighting a losing battle. Her inner mind seemed to have lost its control. Nothing seemed real any more. Ever since the previous evening she had been out of perspective, and she knew there was nothing she could do about it. All she could do was ride out the tempestuous emotions and hope that she would find a safe harbour somewhere on the distant shores of love...

Chapter Three

Going on duty that evening, Lydia found it difficult to concentrate upon what she was doing. Her mind was filled with thoughts of Tim, and she could not chase them into the background where they belonged. All she felt like doing was sitting down at her desk and letting her thoughts have full sway, but she had duties to perform, and she looked around impatiently for Nurse Dillon before setting about her own work.

Nurse Dillon was coming out of one of the patients' rooms on the first floor, and Lydia waited for the girl to come up with her, eyeing her speculatively, and wondering if she had been with Charles that evening. Nurse Dillon smiled at her, and Lydia felt certain that there was a sneer on the girl's face. But it was partly concealed by the smile, and Lydia let it pass. It didn't matter to her that she and Charles were through. In fact she felt as if she had never been out with Charles since her arrival. That was the great effect Tim was having upon her.

'We had two new admissions today, Nurse,' Lydia said. 'One of them is seriously ill, and I want you to keep a close watch on him. He's Mr Barlor, in Room thirty-two! We're doing temperature and pulse checks at thirty-minute intervals.'

'Very good, Sister. At what time shall I make the next check?'

Lydia consulted her watch, then told the girl, and they chatted for some moments about their duties in general. Only the two of them were on duty through the night, and they each had a floor to supervise, with Lydia of course keeping an eye on both floors. There were more than forty patients in the Clinic at this time, some having been operated upon and others recovering from illnesses. The two of them coped quite well, for Nurse Dillon was good at her job and could safely be left to take care of her own duties. But Lydia was concerned about the problem of Charles Powell, and she knew her fears were justified. He would be sneaking around the corridors and looking for the opportunity of distracting Nurse Dillon from her duty.

'I don't want to harp upon what happened last night, Nurse,' she said at length. 'But I would repeat that if you are caught in a compromising situation you'll be for the high jump. I shall have no choice but to make a report of it if I catch you.'

'Don't worry, Sister, it won't happen again. I was taken by surprise last night, but I'll guard against him after this. I don't want to lose my position here!'

Lydia felt that she could believe the girl, but she knew just how persuasive Charles Powell could be and she resolved to remain alert herself. She wouldn't tolerate any kind of deviation from the strict rules. She had never broken the regulations herself, and she would see to it that no one else did!

They parted and went their separate ways, and Lydia made a round of the entire Clinic as was her custom when first taking over. She checked each patient personally, and made a mental note of those patients most likely to require her attention during the night. She finally made her way back to her office, and was surprised to find Charles Powell seated at the desk.

Pausing in the doorway, Lydia stared at him, her surprise showing in her face, and he smiled at her.

'How did you get on this afternoon?' he demanded. 'Saw you going into the village later. It rained before you got back here, didn't it?'

'I got soaked,' she replied, smiling at the recollection. 'But I got a lift back here.'

'Tim Fairfax! I didn't know he was interested in you. Have you been out with him before?'

'Never.'

'Not even when I used to go away for the week-end?' he persisted.

'No. I told you I'd never been out with him. But why the interest?'

'I don't know! Tim never struck me as being a ladies' man. I don't think he's been out with a girl since he came here. You'd better be careful where he is. I've had the feeling for a long time that he's married.'

'Married!' Lydia stared at him aghast. Then she caught her breath and chuckled. 'Surely not! He doesn't seem to leave the Clinic even when he's off duty – not to go away for a week-end or so. His wife would have been much in evidence in the time that he's been here if he were married!'

'Don't be so sure! I wouldn't like to see you getting into deep water, Lydia! You're too nice a girl for that. I'd take you back again rather than see anything come to you!'

'You'd take me back again!' she echoed, and a smile touched her lips. 'You've got more than your share of nerve, Charles.'

'You know what I mean. I have only your best interests at heart. We were friends, Lydia. I don't think I enjoyed our particular relationship with any other girl. You were unique! I still think highly of you, and if I ever want a wife then I'll come back to you!'

She shook her head helplessly, knowing that he was not serious, and she understood more about him now they had parted than she had ever learned when they had been seeing one another.

'Would you like some coffee?' she asked.

'No thanks. I had a whisky a short time ago. I'm going to bed now. Don't do too much, will you?'

She smiled again as he got to his feet, and his face was set in a jocular expression.

'You know me,' she said. 'I'll do whatever I have to.'

'One of the best,' he retorted. 'Don't forget that I've always been keen on you.'

He moved to the door, and paused there to glance at her again. Lydia watched his face, wondering why they had been friends for so long, and yet they had never come to mean anything to one another. He nodded slowly.

'Don't work Diana as hard as you work yourself,' he pleaded. 'She's not as robust as you, and I need her when she's off duty.' He grinned again and departed, and Lydia shook her head slowly as she sat down behind the desk and prepared to do her paperwork.

Midnight came and there was less to do. Lydia brought her desk work up to date and set off on another round of the Clinic. She went looking for Nurse Dillon, and was suspicious until she found the girl. But apparently Nurse Dillon was doing her duty, and there was no sign of Charles Powell anywhere. Lydia relented a little and went on about her own duties.

It was almost twelve-thirty when there was a commotion in the hall near the main entrance, and Lydia seated once more at her desk in the office adjacent to the hall, hurriedly left her seat and went to investigate. She found one of the day nurses just inside the doorway, leaning against the wall and crying in great distress.

Lydia hurried to the girl's side, noting that one of the nurse's shoes was missing, and the girl's legs were covered in mud.

'What's wrong?' Lydia demanded, taking the girl's arm.

Nurse Gerard, a pretty brunette of twenty-four, looked up, her face pale, her shoulders heaving convulsively as she sobbed.

'There was someone out there in the gardens,' she gasped. 'He chased me up the drive!'

'A man!' Lydia went cold for a moment, for she had many times thought how lonely and dark the grounds were at night, and they were remote in this spot.

'Yes, it was a man. I stopped when he called to me, thinking it might be one of our porters, but he grabbed at me, and I dropped my handbag and lost a shoe as I fled from him.'

'I'd better ring the police,' Lydia said. 'Come into the office and I'll get you a cup of coffee.'

'Don't call the police!' Nurse Gerard

pleaded. 'I don't want to get mixed up in anything like this.'

'There's always a risk of this sort of thing happening around a hospital or a Clinic,' Lydia said, shaking her head. 'It's our duty to make a report if there is an incident, no matter how insignificant. You mustn't think of yourself but of the next girl who might cross that man's path.'

She took the girl's arm and led her into the office, making her sit down, and then she telephoned the local police station, giving particulars to the brisk voice at the other end of the line. She was promised a visit by a constable, and hung up to go and make some coffee.

Nurse Gerard was feeling better by the time the policeman arrived, and Lydia was on hand to admit him with the minimum of noise. She led him into the office and he began to question the still shaken girl. Lydia listened carefully, especially when the nurse gave a faint description of the intruder. But it didn't bring anyone to her mind, and she left the policeman to his questioning and made a round of the patients.

When she returned to her office, Lydia found the policeman had almost finished his investigation, and he nodded at her as she paused in the doorway.

'I'll go and take a look around outside, Sister,' he said. 'I should find a shoe and a handbag out there unless robbery wasn't his motive.' He shook his head as he paused. 'We had a spot of bother in the village two nights ago with a similar incident. I hope this isn't a sign that we're in for a spate of these cases.'

'I'm sorry I couldn't be of more help,' Nurse Gerard said hurriedly. 'But it was dark out there, and I was so scared.'

'That's all right. We'll get hold of him, whoever he is!' The constable smiled grimly. 'We usually get them in the end. I may want to talk to you again, Nurse, but I think you've had enough for one night. I'll just try to find your belongings out there. Can you get some footwear and accompany me?'

Nurse Gerard nodded slowly, reluctantly, and she got to her feet and left the office with the constable. Lydia sat down at her desk with a troubled expression on her face, and she considered for a moment the problems that might arise from the incident that had distressed Nurse Gerard.

But the calls of duty soon pushed the thoughts from her mind, and when Nurse Dillon came for her to attend one of the more seriously ill patients, Lydia had no time to consider anything else. The patient, Mrs Terrington, was in a serious condition, having contracted pneumonia after a fall. It seemed that they had won the fight for the ageing woman's life, but the day report had informed Lydia that unexpected complications had set in, and now Lydia found herself with a crisis on her hands.

Tim Fairfax was on first call, and she had no hesitation in sending for him when she found the condition of the patient even more critical. Tim came quickly, his face gaunt, his eyes showing that he had been asleep when the summons came. But he made no fuss, and instantly instructed that an oxygen tent should be rigged up about the patient. Lydia worked with him, and they were silent until they had completed the task. Then Tim examined the woman, and nodded his relief.

'I think we've got her in time,' he said. 'But you're going to have to watch her all the time, Lydia!'

She nodded, liking the sound of her name upon his lips. It was the first time he had called her by her name when on duty, and she felt a thrill touch her at the awareness.

'I'll get Nurse Dillon to watch her, and I'll take over both floors,' Lydia said.

'Can you manage by yourself?' he demanded instantly.

'Oh yes! I frequently take care of the entire establishment.' She smiled. 'It isn't too bad so long as most of the patients sleep the night through.'

He nodded and they walked along to her office. Lydia gave instructions to Nurse

Dillon, who hurried back to Mrs Terrington's room, and for the moment the crisis seemed to be over.

'Would you like some coffee before going back to bed?' Lydia asked. 'I was about to make some before the crisis.'

'Thank you, I think I would like a cup,' Tim replied, and he came to the doorway of the tiny adjacent kitchen and watch Lydia as she boiled the kettle and made the coffee.

She told him about the incident involving Nurse Gerard in the grounds, and Tim's face took on a grim expression as he listened.

'I rather fancied I heard some sort of a commotion outside.' he said. 'My room at the top of the house overlooks the front gardens. But I thought it was the wind. It does howl sometimes around the chimneys. Was she hurt at all?'

'No! The man didn't manage to get hold of her, but it's a nasty business when something like that happens.'

'Did Nurse Gerard get a look at the man?'

'Not clearly. It's really dark out there at

this time of the year. It's a wonder they haven't strung out lamps along the driveway to the house.'

'Perhaps they will now. But you say there was an incident elsewhere in the locality recently?'

'So the constable said. I expect they'll have someone watching the place after this. It's a nerve racking thought that there might be a prowler somewhere out there, watching the place and waiting for some unsuspecting girl.' Lydia suppressed a shudder and sighed.

'Well we shall see to it that you never have to be out there alone,' Tim said, narrowing his blue eyes as he took his coffee from her and led the way back to the office, where he seated himself beside the desk.

Lydia followed him and sat down sighing a little as she tried to relax. Then she glanced as her watch and got up again.

'Please excuse me for a moment,' she said quickly. 'I've got to give Mr Thirtle his injection.'

Tim shook his head as she went to the door, and Lydia smiled as she read his expression of sympathy.

'A nurse's work is never done,' she said lightly as she hurried along the corridor.

After administering the injection to the patient, she went back to the office, to find Tim sagging in the chair with his eyes closed. She paused in the doorway and studied him for a moment, shaking her head as she observed his great tiredness. He didn't get the chance to sleep during the day as the night staff did! She went forward quietly and gently touched his shoulder, starting him awake, and he looked up quickly into her concerned face.

'You'd better be getting back to bed, Tim,' she said softly. 'There's another day to-morrow, remember.'

'Thank goodness there is,' he said with a smile, then stifled a yawn. 'I shall be looking forward to seeing you. But you're right. Sleep is the most important thing on the agenda at the moment. I don't think you'll need to call me in Mrs Terrington's case, Lydia, but don't hesitate to if there's the slightest change in her condition again.'

'I'll be watching her very closely,' Lydia assured him, and he smiled as he got to his feet. For a moment he rested his hands lightly upon her slim shoulders, and she looked up into his face. 'I suppose it is a bit ridiculous to wish you goodnight now,' she said, and saw him nod.

'But say it anyway,' he retorted.

'Goodnight, Tim!'

'Goodnight, Lydia. I hope the morning soon comes for you.' He bent and kissed her lightly on the mouth, and she caught her breath and stifled a gasp as he turned away. He paused in the doorway and looked back at her, smiling, and then he departed, and she sat down at the desk to drink her coffee and bring her reports up to date.

She was filled with a pleasant sense of wellbeing during the rest of the night, and her thoughts, during her free moments, scarcely left Tim. When she was finally relieved she went for breakfast, then took a shower before going to bed, and she was conscious, as she tumbled into bed for a well deserved sleep, that her anticipation of the future was greater than it had ever been before.

When she awakened later, in the early afternoon, she found that rain was beating against the window panes, and she got out of bed and padded to the window. She had no reason to go out, and sat down on the foot of the bed to recollect her sleep-scattered senses. She always experienced a bewildering period upon waking up, and today was no exception. But when her wits returned she began to dress, and her entire outlook was slanted towards the pleasure of seeing Tim again.

When she went along to the dining room for a meal she found Nurse Dillon there, as usual, and they sat together, the girl apparently having got over her sheepishness at the drastic turn of events in Lydia's social life.

'The police have been buzzing around all morning, so I'm told,' Diana Dillon said. 'They want to talk to you, Sister.'

'About that business involving Nurse Gerard?' Lydia shook her head. 'They won't get very far with their investigations if they hope I can help them.'

'I was at a hospital once where we had similar trouble, only the man got right into the nurse's quarters,' Nurse Dillon said. 'That was in the heart of Birmingham, too!' She paused and shrugged her shoulders. 'This place is remote. Just think of the panic there would be if a man got in here.'

'That's not the outlook one should take,' Lydia said sharply. 'Especially as we're on night duty. But I don't think anyone would come into the building. There's a night porter on duty, and two doctors who can be called instantly. How is Nurse Gerard today, anyway?'

'She's still shocked by the whole thing.'

'Has she any idea who the man might be?'

'She said she wouldn't be able to

recognize him again if she saw him. I expect she was too scared to even think of looking at him.'

Lydia nodded. 'You're off duty tonight, Nurse,' she said, changing the subject. 'Nurse Gerard is due to come on in your place.'

'I'm thinking of asking to be transferred to day shift,' Nurse Dillon said.

'Oh!' Lydia shook her head. 'I thought you were happy working with me.'

'I am, and I've always preferred night to day shift, but there are other reasons, Sister.' Her face turning red, Nurse Dillon tried to smile unconcernedly.

'I see!' Lydia smiled. 'Well it's none of my business, of course, but I would warn you to be careful where Doctor Powell is concerned. It may not last! You wouldn't be the first girl to think she had captured him, only to find herself empty handed at the end. Don't think it's sour grapes with me, Nurse. I was never in love with Charles. We were just good friends.'

'I believe you, Sister.' The girl nodded seriously. 'I've been worried that perhaps I took him away from you, but he did start paying attention to me on the quiet. I thought you were too nice a person to be deceived by him, so I'm glad you found out about him as soon as you did.'

'You go right ahead and win him if you can,' Lydia told her. 'Shall I make a report to Matron that you'd like to go back on days? I'm sure she'll arrange it from the end of the week. Normally we all take turns on night shift, as you know, but no-one objects if one desires to remain on permanent night duty.'

'I think I'd like a change for a bit, Sister.'

'Very well, I'll see what I can do to arrange it.'

They parted then, and Lydia began to think of the coming evening. She knew Tim would be off duty from six, and that would give them a little time together. She could understand why Nurse Dillon wanted to get back on day duty. It would enable her to spend a full evening with Charles Powell, instead of having to cut most evenings short in order to get back to the Clinic in time for duty. She wondered about herself, and made a mental note to talk to Tim about going back on day duty.

When she returned to her room Lydia found herself thinking deeply about Tim. The fact that they were only now going out together made no difference to her outlook. It wasn't as if they were strangers. They had known one another for eight months! But in that time they had been on formal terms, and she was still finding it difficult to think of him in any other way.

Yet she knew she was attracted to him, powerfully and completely. She trembled inside when she thought of him, and she knew that this was the nearest she had ever been to love. It was uncanny how the situation had developed so quickly, but she knew now that Tim had only been waiting for his chance to speak to her. He hadn't made a move while she had been out with Charles.

She knew she wanted the situation to develop still more! Her whole being cried with every nerve she possessed. She wanted romance and love. She wanted a man like Tim, for she realized now that he was her ideal man. That was why she had taken to him so quickly when he made his own feelings known. She had subconsciously recognized him as a most important being.

It seemed that getting to know Tim like this had changed the course of her whole life, and Lydia could not argue against the pointers that seemed to be directing her. She had never known what it was like to be in love, but she was filled now with a crazy series of subconscious longings and thoughts. All she could really tell was that she wanted to fall in love, and she hoped Tim would prove to be the right man.

Chapter Four

Days passed in a long round of night duty and days of sleeping. The only thing that showed progress was the situation between Tim and Lydia, and at the end of the first week of their going out together Lydia was certain she was in love with him.

She learned a lot about Tim in that week, and a comfortable atmosphere surrounded them. Other events at the Clinic did not seem to touch Lydia, and she was quite content with her own small world of rosy love.

But Charles Powell was industrious in his pursuit of pleasure, and when Diana Dillon changed over to day duties, Christine Gerard, now recovered from her shocking experience with the unknown prowler took over as Lydia's assistant.

Lydia found Nurse Gerard a very efficient girl, and they got on well together. It was easy to see that the girl had suffered a great shock that night she had been accosted, and she never tired of talking about it or wondering if the police had discovered the identity of the man responsible. Lydia did what she could to help the girl get over her shock, but it seemed that time itself would have to take care of the situation.

Then Lydia found Charles Powell chasing after Nurse Gerard, and she was worried for several nights while she puzzled what to do. Her first intimation of history repeating itself was when she walked past an empty room on the first floor, where Nurse Gerard was on duty. Looking for the girl to check with her, Lydia failed to find her in the small office, and was walking silently back towards the stairs when she heard the muted sounds of voices nearby and traced them to the empty room. She knew before she pushed open the door of the room that one of the occupants would be Charles, and she was not wrong.

Opening the door quickly and silently, Lydia saw Nurse Gerard standing by the foot of the bed, her hands lifted to Powell's shoulders, and Charles was looking earnestly into the girl's brown eyes. Nurse Gerard saw Lydia first, and her face changed expression instantly as she stepped away from the handsome doctor. Charles looked around instinctively, and a crooked smile touched his good-looking face as he saw Lydia.

'You'd better get about your duties, Nurse,' Lydia said firmly.

Nurse Gerard nodded instantly and hurried from the room in great relief. Powell changed his position and came towards Lydia, still smiling.

'You're getting to be quite a detective,' he said. 'Why are you chasing the nurses around? Are you sorry already that we parted?'

'Charles, I don't understand you! You never used to be so brazen. You know you could get that nurse into a lot of trouble, bringing her into a room like this while she's still on duty.'

'I imagine she'd get into a lot of trouble if I brought her into this room when she was off duty,' he retorted with a cheeky grin.

'What's happened to Nurse Dillon? She changed her duties in order to be off duty in the evenings with you.'

'I saw her this evening,' he said. 'But I like Christine Gerard, and she seems willing to be friendly. Anything to help relieve the loneliness of this place.'

'It's none of my business what you do or with whom you go while you and the nurses are off duty, Charles.' Lydia tried to make her tones harsh. 'But while a nurse is on duty with me she's not going to get up to this sort of thing. It's the second time I've caught you like this, and if it happens again I'm going to make a report to Matron.'

'You didn't catch me the first time,' he protested, grinning at her. 'I do believe you're jealous of these other girls, because we're not seeing each other again. I can't accept that you would prefer Tim Fairfax to me!'

'How vain can you get?' Lydia demanded, getting angry because he was mocking her. 'I'm serious in what I say. You'd lose your position here if I did make a report to Matron! Have some sense, Charles, and start acting your age. These nurses aren't here for your benefit, you know.'

'Aren't they?' He was still smiling. He came closer to her, and reached out for her shoulders before she realized what he was doing. 'I've always had a soft spot for you, Lydia, you know. I would give up all the other girls just for the chance to get back with you again.'

She pushed his hands away, stiffening herself. 'Don't touch me,' she warned. 'You're going too far, Charles, and you must know. I don't know what's come over you. This sort of behaviour can only make trouble for you, so without what may happen to the nurses involved. Can't you find the right girl to settle with?'

'I'm too young to think of settling,' he retorted lightly. 'I have always played the field. You go on about your duties, Lydia, and leave me to take care of my own problems.'

'Have you got problems?' she demanded.

He smiled and shook his head. 'That was the wrong word to use,' he said.

'Well it is my business when you're preventing one of my nurses from concentrating upon her duties, and this is the last time I shall overlook it. If it happens again I shall certainly bring the matter to Matron's attention.'

'Just as you will!' he turned away from her, but then swung back to seize hold of her and hold her tightly. The next instant he was kissing her, and Lydia was too surprised to struggle for the moment. Before she could resist, there was a sound in the doorway, and Lydia wrenched herself free of him to turn and see Nurse Gerard watching them with surprise on her face.

Lydia was speechless with shock, and she could only stare at the girl, whose face showed that she would have a pretty tale to relate. Charles smiled as he went towards the girl.

'You ought to have more sense than to come bursting into a room like that, Nurse,' he rebuked lightly. 'That's Sister Redmond's habit!'

'I'm sorry, Doctor, but one of my patients is having a bad turn. Would you come quickly?'

'Certainly! Who is it?'

'Mrs Addison!' Nurse Gerard glanced at Lydia and then turned and hurried out. Charles followed her, and Lydia took a deep breath and tried to recover her self-control before following in their footsteps.

Fighting down her anger, Lydia went into the patient's room, to find Charles handling the situation. She remained in the background, knowing he would call her forward if he needed her, but he addressed himself to Nurse Gerard, and Lydia felt that he was ignoring her deliberately.

Nurse Gerard departed to prepare an injection, and Charles remained attending the patient. When the nurse returned the injection was administered, which quickly settled the patient, and then Charles spoke in an undertone to Nurse Gerard before turning away from the bed and coming towards Lydia.

'Shall we go into your office to talk?' he asked pleasantly, although he subjected her to a searching stare.

'There's nothing more to be said,' she retorted, shaking her head, still feeling angry at the way he had handled her. 'I've had my say, and I shan't repeat any of it. But be warned, Charles. I shall have no hesitation in doing my duty if I catch you again.'

'I'll be in my quarters if you should need me again during the night,' he said, smiling, and he walked past her and set off along the corridor.

Lydia felt the impulse to chase after him

and try to smash his self assurance. But she merely moved into the doorway in order to watch his departure. When he had gone she turned to find Nurse Gerard standing by the foot of the patient's bed, watching her with some apprehension, and Lydia nodded slowly as their eyes met.

'Yes, Nurse, I wish to talk to you,' she said. 'Let us go along to the office.'

'I don't see what there is to talk about,' came the pert reply. 'I have only to tell what I saw and you'll lose your job here, Sister.'

'I doubt that very much when I give my own account of what happened. You know as well as I do that Doctor Powell seized hold of me because he heard your approach. He wanted to set up this situation so you could blackmail me against talking. Well it won't work, and if I have the slightest reason to suspect that you're not doing your duty properly at any time during the night then I shall have no hesitation in reporting the matter, notwithstanding what may happen to me.'

'Very well, Sister. I promise you that it won't happen again.'

'I shall be around to see that it doesn't,' Lydia said sharply. 'Now you'd better get round your patients.'

The girl nodded and walked by her, and Lydia watched her for a moment, her brown eyes narrowed and her mind working over the situation like a dog worrying a favourite bone.

She didn't know what had come over Charles Powell! There had been rumours about him from the very moment Lydia had arrived, but she had placed no faith in any of them because she knew how nurses could talk, and especially about a doctor as handsome as Charles Powell. He had acted fairly straight while they had been seeing each other, Lydia recalled, but in the few days since they had parted he'd seemed to become a different man altogether.

Lydia went back to her office, intent upon her duties, but her mind was worrying over the incidents that had occurred. Twice

Charles had deliberately broken the regulations, first with Diana Dillon and now with Christine Gerard. It didn't make sense, for nothing could come of such incidents but trouble for all concerned. Whether he had taken the chance because he fancied that she wouldn't have the nerve to report him to Matron she didn't know, but he would find the lie to that if he made a third attempt to interfere with their line of duty.

Charles was on call that night, and Lydia spent the rest of her time hoping that she wouldn't have to send for him. The night passed slowly, with high winds and heavy rain tormenting the darkness outside. Dawn came late and Lydia was glad to be able to hand over to her relief. She went to her room with the knowledge that she was off duty the next night, and she could begin to plan what to do with her free time.

After her sleep for the day, Lydia awoke with the feeling that something good was going to happen to her. She first sensed her elation when she sat up in the bed and listened intently to discover if it was raining outside. She heard the wind, but the windows were not reporting the ghostly fingers of raindrops, and she jumped out of bed to take a look.

Leaves were blowing from the trees in the grounds, and the bare branches were whipping back and forth under the invisible powers of the wind. It looked a dreary afternoon, but in Lydia's mind there was plenty of sunlight for her to bask in, and she went back to her bed and sat upon it for a moment while she tried to remember what it was Tim had said about today. Then it came back to her and she smiled.

They were both off duty for the rest of the day and Tim had asked her to go for a long drive with him. The weather was such that they could do little else but drive, and Lydia really didn't care what they did so long as she was in his splendid company.

She thought of him as she sat on her bed, and her mind was filled with speculation. Each day found her in similar mood, and each day pushed her a little nearer to admitting her love for him. But she was reluctant to spread her feelings out for close inspection. If it turned out that her emotions were falling short of the real thing then her whole future would turn bleak, and she was scared to face the prospect. Rather to go on living in a fool's paradise for a few more weeks than learn the stark and cold truth. She suppressed a shiver and hastened to dress, going down to the dining hall for her meal and finding Nurse Gerard seated there in place of Nurse Dillon.

Lydia studied the girl's face and found sheepishness in her expression. It reminded Lydia of the time she had found out about Charles and Diana Dillon. History was repeating itself already! But she hoped there would not be a third time, for the girl's sake as well as Charles Powell's.

'Hello, Sister, had a good sleep?' Nurse Gerard demanded a trifle awkwardly, and Lydia smiled as she nodded. She had no intention of making the girl squirm.

'I slept quite well,' she replied. 'You'll have Sister Eaton with you tonight. I'm off duty.'

'I'd rather be working with you,' came the surprising reply, and Lydia showed some of her surprise. 'I mean that, despite what happened last night,' the girl continued. 'You're the best Sister on the staff.'

'You must think yourself very fortunate that it was me who caught you last night in that compromising situation,' Lydia said slowly. 'If it had been Nurse Eaton you would have left here this morning.'

'I know, Sister, and I'm very sorry about it. But I was taken unawares in much the same way that you were.' A faint smile touched the girl's lips, and Lydia nodded, recalling her anger at being caught out by Charles Powell.

'Then let's forget about it this time, shall we?' she invited, and was relieved when the girl nodded. 'But you are not the first girl I've caught with Doctor Powell,' she added meaningly. 'Don't let him kid you it is the first time he's ever done anything like that.'

'I heard about Nurse Dillon,' came the surprising retort, and Lydia began to eat her meal, her mind upon Charles, with Tim fighting for notice from the background of her mind.

Nurse Gerard left shortly after, and Lydia hastened to finish her meal. She was about to leave the dining room when Tim appeared, and she knew instantly by his face that something was wrong. She froze a little inside, wondering how his next words would affect her.

'I'm sorry, Lydia, about today,' he said as soon as he saw her. 'Powell has asked me to take over his duties today. He's got to go down to London.'

'What's happened?' she demanded.

'Some emergency, so Powell says. He wouldn't ask me to switch duties like this if it were not important. Naturally I agreed to stand in for him, and that means we're going to miss our time together.'

'There'll be other times,' she responded instantly. 'I'm sorry that we shan't be able to get together, but it isn't the end of the world, is it?'

They were alone now in the dining room, and Tim sat down beside her and took her hands in his.

'I can tell that you're greatly disappointed,' he said happily. 'It's a good sign, Lydia. I cursed my luck when Powell approached me, but there was nothing I could do.'

'He hasn't dreamed up this emergency to prevent us going out together for the day, has he?' she demanded.

Tim looked into her face without blinking, and she saw a shadow come to his face. Then he shook his head.

'Why should he do that?' he demanded. 'It's all over between you two, isn't it?'

'There was never anything between us that could come to an end,' she replied.

'That's what I thought. I know Powell very well. I've had the chance to study him lately, and I don't think he could be serious about any girl. But has he said anything to you since we've been seeing each other, Lydia?'

'About us?' She shook her head. 'No. He never cared for me enough to wonder what I'm doing now, although he's heard about us.'

Tim nodded, his face reflective.

'So this emergency of his will be genuine. I'm sorry it's come to upset our day, Lydia. I've been looking forward to this.'

'Never mind!' Her face showed that she was disappointed, and he sighed heavily as he squeezed her hands intimately.

'What do you usually do with yourself when you're off duty, before we started going together, I mean. You didn't spend much time with Powell, except in the evenings.'

'I never did much but stay around here,' she said.

'Can you drive?'

'Yes, although I haven't done so since I've been here. I do have a clean licence!' She smiled at him, and he nodded.

'Well my car is insured for any driver. The

tank is filled ready for today, so why not take yourself off somewhere? It will make a nice change for you.'

'I wouldn't feel happy on my own, knowing that we were to have been together,' she protested.

'Nonsense. You'll feel a lot worse hanging around here. We can always get out together later.'

'I must say the prospect it tempting,' Lydia said slowly.

'There you are then! Go and get ready and I'll see you in thirty minutes. I'll show you the controls on the car and you can drive off to where ever you please. No doubt you have some shopping you want to do.' He grinned. 'I don't want to see you on that cycle ever again.'

She smiled at the recollection. 'Cycling is very good for the figure,' she retorted.

'There's nothing wrong with your figure the way it is.'

'I promise not to use the cycle again.' She was smiling, and suddenly there was a warm emotion inside her and she wanted to push herself into his arms and be kissed. She glanced around the room, and was glad it was deserted. Getting to her feet, she pulled him upright and pushed herself into his arms.

'Lydia!' He whispered her name huskily, and hugged her with great strength. 'What a girl you are! I still can't believe that at last you're seeing me. It was a nightmare while you went around with Powell, and I used to curse my luck! To think that he wasn't serious about you and I couldn't let you know what my feelings are!'

'It must have been dreadful for you, Tim,' she said. 'And you didn't give me the slightest hint. Whenever we spoke or met you were always meticulously formal.'

'I had to hold myself at a distance, Lydia,' he retorted. 'I didn't dare let you see what my feelings were.'

'But you're serious about me!' She looked up into his face, with tenderness in her own expression, and he smiled and nodded.

'I love you, Lydia,' he admitted gently. 'I've loved you for a long time.'

She regarded him intently, looking into his eyes, and she could tell that he was speaking the truth. The knowledge sent a thrill through her. Her own emotions were aroused, but she could not with any truth decide what she really felt for him. He attracted her! He seemed to fill her with indescribable emotions, some of which she had never experienced before, and it would have been too easy to lump them all together and call the encompassing result love! But she wanted to analyze herself, to be perfectly certain that it was love before she admitted it.

'I can see something of a struggle going on inside you,' he said observantly. 'Don't try to force any decision from your own mind. Let it come naturally. I want you to love me, but I'm prepared to wait for you to discover your real feelings. I can't say fairer than that. I want you to do the right thing, and do it naturally. At the same time I know my own mind sufficiently to realize that it will never change, so I think you ought to know exactly how I feel about you.'

She could feel great pressures building up in her mind, and her desires seemed to be getting out of hand. She tilted her face and moistened her lips.

'Kiss me, Tim,' she commanded, and he smiled gently and obeyed.

But it was not the time or the place for such a show of loving tenderness, and Lydia was afraid they might be surprised by one of the maids. She sighed deeply as she pushed herself away from him, and her eyes were glowing from inner fires as she moved to the door.

'I'd like nothing better than to be in your company today, Tim. I shall hardly be able to wait until next time.'

'It will come,' he said realistically. 'But you go and change, and I'll look for you out at my car in about thirty minutes. The temptation to go with you will he unbearable, but we can wait. One thing we have is time on our side.

She nodded and they left the dining room, to part at the stairs, Tim going along to the office and Lydia hurrying up to her room. She didn't know what to do with her time, but she realized that Tim had spoken the truth. She would be frustrated and lonely at the Clinic, knowing that they should have been out together. If she took out his car she would at least get some benefit from being off duty.

When she went down later she found Tim standing by the main entrance, talking to Matron, and he looked up at her and smiled, the simple expression of delight at seeing her sending a pang through her heart. She approached him as if walking on air, and Matron went off discreetly after greeting Lydia.

'You look first class!' Tim said, taking her arm as he opened the door. 'I wish I could go with you for even a short drive, but I've got to stand by. As you know, there are several patients who are on the Seriously Ill list, and duty comes first.'

She nodded. 'Look, Tim, I'd stay in if I thought we could spend some time together.'

'I'd like nothing better, but I want you to go because if you stay here it will he too great a temptation for me to remain away from you. I'm on duty, although you're not, and it wouldn't do for us to be together under those circumstances.'

'That's quite true, unfortunately,' she retorted.

'So take my car and go for a long drive. Enjoy yourself, Lydia. Have a nice time. You are a really hard working girl and you need some relaxation.'

'Yes, Doctor!' she said in the tones a patient might use, and he sighed heavily and squeezed her arm as they walked across the gravelled drive to the car.

Tim drove a white Fiat 124, and Lydia found that the controls were quite simple and regular. They sat together in the car for a few moments, and Tim held her hand tightly. Lydia felt reluctant to leave him. But he was insistent, and she knew she would have to go and leave him behind.

'Drive carefully until you get used to the clutch and the accelerator,' he warned. 'You shouldn't need any petrol – the tank is filled. Have you any money in case you should?'

'Yes!' She smiled as she nodded. 'You're not going to subsidize my outing.'

'I shall!' He spoke firmly, then leaned towards her and kissed her tenderly.

'Oh, Tim!' His name was forced from her lips, and she experienced a wonderful sensation deep inside.

'Lydia! I love you!' His face was serious as he looked at her, then he sighed and jerked open the door at his side. 'I'd better let you get away or I shall keep you here all afternoon. I hope you'll have a nice time. I shall be thinking of you, and do be careful on the roads. I personally don't subscribe to general male attitude towards women drivers, and I'm not concerned for the car. Take care of yourself, my love!'

She was surprised to experience a trembling inside, and she clung to him for a moment, her mind dilating under the growing pressures of love.

'Tim, I'm sure I love you!' she said in an agonized whisper.

'Tell me all about it later,' he said, and there was an eager note in his voice. He kissed her again and then got out of the car. 'Be careful,' he called, and she nodded.

'I'll bring the car back in one piece,' she promised.

He stepped back and she started the engine, and for a moment she hesitated, finding a great division of intention in her mind. Then she let in the clutch and drove away rather neatly, glancing in the rear mirror to see that Tim was waving and smiling his approval.

Lydia felt like a bird escaping from a cage as she left the grounds, although she would have been a great deal happier had Tim been with her. But she drove along the road that led to town with an overpowering sensation of elation in her mind. She tried to dismiss it, wanting to concentrate upon her driving until she became really familiar with the car.

She noticed a blue Mini behind her as soon as she left the Clinic, and several times on the way to town she slowed to let it pass her, but the driver remained well back, and she smiled to herself as she imagined that he might be too wary to pass a woman driver on such a narrow, winding road. She had no clear idea of what she was going to do, but the novelty of driving herself was too pleasant to be wasted, and she intended taking full advantage of the situation!

Chapter Five

Lydia didn't stay long in town. She drove in to make some purchases and then went on for a drive relishing the loneliness because it gave her the opportunity to think without interruption, but she felt sad that Tim was not with her. When it began to rain she drove carefully, and liked the wet weather because she was so snug and warm inside the car.

When the light began to fail she pulled into a village and went to look for a restaurant, and found a small place on the main street. She went in and ordered a pot of tea and some sandwiches. Rain was still beating against the windows, and Lydia could not take her mind from thoughts of Tim. If only they were together now! She felt desire building up inside her, and she clenched her hands as she tried to contain it. She had never felt like this before, and she was more than a little shaken by the powerful emotions.

If this was what being in love was like then she would be happy for the rest of her life. The thought was vibrant in her mind and she kept sighing and hoping, wishing and praying that what seemed about to come true for her would not fade away before it became reality.

She was disturbed by someone standing over her, and when she dragged herself from her thoughts she found herself looking up at a rather pleasant young man.

'Would you mind if I sat with you?' he asked.

Lydia looked around at the other empty tables, and did not reply immediately, but he sensed what was in her mind and smiled disarmingly.

'Sorry if I appear to be trying to pick you up, but you do work at the Pinewood Clinic, don't you?'

'Yes, I do! How do you know?'

'I live in that area myself, and I know some of the staff who work there.' He paused. 'I'm Terry Craig!'

'I see.' Lydia sighed and moved her bag off the table. 'Sit down by all means!'

He had a pot of tea, and sat opposite, chatting quickly, as if hoping to break the ice between them. He knew Nurse Kent and Nurse Gerard, he said, and Lydia felt easier as she listened to him.

'I saw you leaving the Clinic this afternoon in the white Fiat, didn't I?' he demanded at length.

'I am driving a white Fiat,' she admitted.

'I drive a blue Mini.'

'I saw you on the road just after I came out of the Clinic!' Lydia frowned as she recalled the car that had refused to overtake her. 'Was it you driving?'

'Yes. I must admit that I've been following you, trying to summon up courage to talk to you, and when you came in here I felt it was too good a chance to miss.'

'Really!' Lydia said in more formal tones.

'I didn't mean any harm by it,' he said quickly. He was in his early twenties, she guessed, studying his rather pale face. His eyes were blue, and seemed troubled, filled with apprehension, and Lydia sensed that he had been ill, judging by his general appearance.

'Oh, that's all right,' she said. 'Where do you live, by the way?'

'In Norton.'

'I see! How well do you know the nurses at the Clinic?'

'I've taken Christine Gerard out several times. She's a nice girl! What's she like as a nurse?'

'Very good!' Lydia answered his questions, and he went on to ask many questions about the clinic and the staff working there. He seemed to know a great deal about the place already, and despite the fact that Lydia didn't like the way he had approached her, she found he had an engaging personality, and was quite pleasant to talk to.

But eventually she decided it was time to leave, and she took up her handbag.

'Do you have to go yet?' he demanded anxiously. 'The evening is still early. We could go for a drive in my car or yours, and continue this chat we're having.'

'I'm sorry, but it isn't early for me,' Lydia replied. 'I have to get back in order to go on duty later.' She felt justified in telling a white lie because she sensed that she might have difficulty in getting away from him.

'I see! That's a pity.' He waved a long, slender hand, and his fingers were very long and artistic. 'Perhaps I can see you some other time?'

'That's not possible.'

'There's someone else?' His blue eyes narrowed, and seemed to turn cold. 'You used to go around with Doctor Powell, but I understand that he's interested in one of the other nurses now!'

'He's interested in more than one of the other nurses,' Lydia said with a smile. 'But you seem to be very well informed about life at the Clinic.'

'I've always been interested in that sort of thing. I sometimes wish I could have been a doctor. But apart from that I was very ill at one time, and I spent a considerable amount of time in a hospital. I like nurses. I think they do a wonderful job.'

Lydia nodded, feeling more friendly towards him now, but she had no intention of spending the rest of the evening with him. He seemed a nice person, but there was something in his free and easy manner that did not sit well with her. She listened to the dictates of her conscience and decided to leave him. He might prove to be an embarrassment if he thought he was becoming friendly.

'I really must go now,' she said at length. 'It's been very nice chatting to you, Terry, but I can't stay any longer.'

'May I see you again?' he demanded, getting to his feet as she arose to leave.

'I'm sorry, but I'm afraid that isn't possible.'

'You haven't found anyone else since Doctor Powell, have you?'

Lydia did not answer, but opened the door of the shop and walked out to the darkness of the pavement. He followed her to the car, and she trembled somewhat convulsively as she unlocked the door.

'I would like to see you again,' he said eagerly. 'Surely we can meet if you get some free time later. You're on permanent night duty, aren't you? I don't work, so we could meet during the day if you're afraid to see me after dark!'

'Why should I be afraid to see you after dark?' she demanded, pausing before getting into the car.

'Well we are strangers, and a girl cannot be too careful these days.'

Lydia thought of the man who had chased Nurse Gerard in the Clinic grounds, and she shook her head.

'It's kind of you to think that I might be lonely off duty, but I'm afraid I can't see you again.'

He shrugged and stepped back, and Lydia opened the car door and got into the vehicle with a sigh of relief. But he remained standing there, his face a pale blur in the shadows, and Lydia felt ashamed of herself for treating him too sharply when he had been pleasant and friendly. She wound down the window and spoke to him.

'Thanks for being so friendly,' she said. 'I have enjoyed talking to you.'

'Then let's talk some more. Drive me back to the Clinic now and I can collect my car from here later.'

'But how will you get back here? It's all of twenty miles from the Clinic!'

'I'll get back! I'd like to go with you.'

'It wouldn't be worth your trouble!' Lydia was surprised by his intentions. She couldn't really believe that he was serious.

'Well make a date to see me again some other time,' he insisted.

'No, I'm sorry!' She shook her head decisively. 'Look, it's beginning to rain really hard again. If you've been ill recently then you'd better get into your car and keep dry.'

'All right.' He was reluctant to go, but he could see the sense of what she said. 'Perhaps I'll see you again.' He turned away quickly, and Lydia found herself staring at his back as he hurried away.

She was thoughtful as she closed the window and prepared to drive away, but before she could move away from the kerb a Mini shot past her at a terrific rate, and she saw it was the one she'd seen upon leaving the Clinic earlier that afternoon. She winced as it went on its way at frightening speed, and when its tyres squealed she thought there was going to be an accident. But the little car went on and vanished into the night, its rear lights gleaming, the brake lights flickering from time to time.

Lydia followed on slowly, and she found herself thinking a great deal about Terry Craig. He seemed a strange young man, most intent and intense, and she could not accept that part of his manner had been natural. But she soon forgot him as she drove back to the Clinic, and her thoughts turned to Tim again.

The night was dark and wet about her, and Lydia felt relaxed and calm as she drove on. Coming out alone had done a lot for her peace of mind, she realized. It had made quite a change to drive herself, and although she would have been much happier with Tim along, she appreciated the solitude and enjoyed it.

When she came in sight of the Clinic she slowed the car, turning into the drive and letting her mind start taking up the normal thoughts that attended her life here. She parked by the side door and hurriedly left the car, running for the shelter of the house because rain was still pelting down, and she jingled Tim's keys as she went in search of him.

Tim was in the small office where the doctors spent most of their time on duty, and he got quickly to his feet when Lydia entered the room after tapping at the door. He came around the desk and swept her into his arms, hugging her tightly as if they had been apart for months. She glanced at the clock on the wall, surprised to find that the time was almost ten.

'Well?' he demanded. 'Have you enjoyed yourself? My thoughts have been with you all the time. I must have wished a thousand times that I could have been with you!'

'It would have been better if you'd been with me,' she replied. 'But it did make a nice change, Tim.'

'Good. It's just what the doctor ordered for you.' He smiled. 'How does it feel to know that a man is in love with you?' he asked. He spoke lightly, but there was seriousness in his face, and Lydia felt her pulses leap as she watched his features.

'I've been thinking of you the whole time,' she said. 'I must have wished two thousand times that you were with me.'

He nodded. 'I know how you feel,' he said. 'Next time we shall be together.'

He kissed her, and Lydia found herself responding in a manner she didn't think she had in her. She clung to him and held on as if for dear life, and he was smiling gently when they finally parted.

'I never thought it could happen to me,' he said simply. 'Yet the first time I set eyes on you I told myself that you were more than average. There's not another girl can compare with you, Lydia.'

'That is how I feel about you,' she said intently.

He took his car keys from her and dropped them into his pocket. She clung tightly to his other hand, and he smiled as he looked into her eyes.

'My darling!' He spoke in a whisper, and she tingled at the huskiness in his tones. 'I love you so very much, and yet it seems incredible to me that I can tell you so. I thought Powell would recognize his good fortune and hang on to you. I wake up in the night sometimes, wondering if this is all true or just a dream. I fully expect you to tell me sometime in the future that there could not possibly be anything in the future for us together.'

She shook her head, pressing her face against his shoulder when he smiled. She could feel warm emotion inside her, and although she had never been in love before she felt certain that it was love she was experiencing. It was so powerful and exquisite. True love couldn't have a greater intensity because the human breast would never be able to encompass it! She breathed deeply and gripped his upper arms with her long fingers, and he stroked her hair, kissing the top of her head, murmuring sweet words in her car.

'I've never been happier,' she said. 'Just knowing you like this has made me realize how empty my previous life has been, Tim. I wish I had met you years ago!'

'I have the same longings,' he admitted. 'It proves that we do feel the same way about one another. Let's go to Wimbledon next week, Lydia, I want you to meet my parents, and I certainly want to meet yours.'

'That's an idea. Shall we visit your parents

first, or mine?'

'We'll toss for it,' he retorted, laughing. 'We can't see them both in the same day, so we'll have to spread the visits over two weeks. I'm beginning to feel like a schoolboy with the school holidays looming over the horizon. Oh, Lydia, I love you so much it hurts.'

He was serious about his feelings, and the knowledge gave her a thrill. How could she have spent eight months here without feeling the slightest thing for him? Surely there ought to have been some sign for either of them to recognize! If Fate had planned this for them and intended that they should continue going together then neither of them had anything to fear. Time would take its course and everything would work out inevitably.

There was a tap at the door, and Lydia started nervously, so intent upon him had she been. He went to the door and opened it, blocking the caller's view into the office, and she heard one of the nurses talking softly. Then he closed the door and sighed heavily as he turned to her.

'I've got to go and take a look at Mrs Terrington,' he said. 'That poor woman's condition is up and down all day and night.'

'But she is making overall progress, isn't she?' Lydia demanded.

'Slowly but surely. The thing is, are we going to be able to bring her through this present series of crises?'

Lydia felt her cheerfulness evaporate as she began to think of duty. As a nurse of long experience she knew she had to forget what happened while she was on duty or she would never have peace of mind. But at times the two different worlds overlapped and some anguish made itself felt. There were some cases which seemed more poignant than others, although each case had its own emotion. Now she felt her mind dilate as she considered the plight of some of their patients, and she tried to fight off the pity that surged upwards in her mind. She felt guilty because she was now so happy, when there were people about them suffering pain and illness. She had a great future to look forward to, and some of their patients were waiting for death to release them for their strictures.

'I'd better go, Lydia,' Tim said, smiling gently. He put an arm about her shoulder and led her to the door. 'See you tomorrow sometime. We'll go out tomorrow evening for a bit, shall we?'

'Yes please!' She sighed deeply and then drew a shuddering breath as she tried to control her emotions. 'See you tomorrow, Tim.'

He paused before opening the door and drew her once more into his arms, and when he kissed her, slowly and tenderly, she felt as if her mind was under attack. Strange sensations got right down into the very roots of her being, and when they finally parted she swayed unsteadily.

'You're beginning to look tired,' he said. 'Go and get a good night's sleep, my dearest.'

She nodded and walked unsteadily away from him, intent upon following his advice, and now she was feeling very tired and wanted nothing more than to slip into bed and let her consciousness founder beneath the onset of slumber.

'Sister!' A voice called to Lydia as she started up the front stairs, and she turned to see Nurse Gerard approaching. 'There was a telephone call for you a few moments ago, Sister,' the girl went on. 'Someone seemed to think you were on duty tonight.'

'A telephone call for me?' Lydia demanded in great surprise. 'You're joking, Nurse!'

'I'm not, Sister,' the girl replied in sharp tones that left Lydia in no doubt. 'I couldn't tell you who it was, but a man's voice asked for the Sister on night duty, and when I passed the call to Sister Eaton she listened for a moment and then hung up. She said something about the call being for you. I just thought I'd let you know in case it was something you were waiting for.'

'But I don't know any man who would call me!' Lydia said.

'Could it have been your father then? Is there some emergency at home?'

'Father would have asked for me by name! You said this caller didn't!'

'That's right, Sister. Is it some unknown admirer that you've just met?'

Lydia shook her head and went on up the stairs, her mind thinking swiftly, and she was almost into her room before she thought of the young man she had spoken to in the restaurant. She paused as she recalled the incident, and her eyes narrowed. What had he said his name was? She frowned as she tried to recall it, and then it came into her mind. Terry Craig! But surely he wouldn't have the nerve to ring her here! She remembered that she had told him she was on duty this evening, and a shaft of pure worry touched the outer edges of her mind as she considered that he might make himself a nuisance.

She went to bed slowly, lost in conjecture,

and she could not help worrying about that strange young man. He had seemed too intense at the time, she thought grimly. But then he had said he'd been ill, and she had made allowances for him because of it. She did know illness, and she was well aware of the effects that some illnesses could have upon a patient.

It took her quite a time to drift into slumber, and then she slept uneasily, as if labouring in the shadow of some unknown premonition. When morning came she awoke to find the day dull and grey, and there seemed to be an intolerable burden on her slim shoulders.

She never liked the day after a night off because it meant that she had to sleep at some time during the afternoon in order to be ready for duty during the coming night. Normally she slept all morning and until two in the afternoon after coming off night duty, but today she would have to change her routine and sleep in the afternoon. It had always been a trial to her, but today she realized that it would become even worse. There was worry in her mind and she could not eject it.

After breakfast she considered what to do with her morning, and had started doing her odd jobs when there was a tap at her door. Opening the door, she found one of the maids standing there, with a message for her to go and see Tim. Thanking the girl, Lydia frowned and went back into the room to make herself presentable, then hurried down to Tim's office.

'Hello, Lydia, did you have a good night?' Tim demanded as soon as she walked in upon him.

'I slept a bit uneasily,' she replied. 'Is anything wrong?'

'Wrong?' He smiled as he shook his head. 'No. I knew you have this morning off duty, and no doubt you'll sleep this afternoon, so I thought you'd run an errand for me into town. Now I know you can drive I'm going to try and make use of you. You're not doing anything special this morning, are you?'

'Nothing at all. What can I do for you?'

'That's what I like to hear!' He took her hand for a moment. He seemed very light hearted and gay, and Lydia felt her mind open even more in his favour. 'Take the car and go into town Lydia, please,' he said. 'There's a parcel for us at the bus station. I said I'd go in and pick it up, but I am too busy to leave right now.' He held out his car keys, and Lydia smiled as she took them.

'Certainly I'll go,' she said. 'But I have the feeling you are going to get me to drive when we go out together in an evening.'

'That's certainly an idea,' he retorted, and squeezed her hand. 'Are we going out for a drive this evening?'

'Yes please.' She nodded eagerly, and he studied her face for a moment.

'It's a pity that there's nothing much else we can do except go for a drive,' he said. 'Now in London there would be a great many diversions for us.'

'I wouldn't thank you for London,' she retorted, shaking her head. 'I'd settle for a lonely drive with you at any time.'

He nodded slowly, and his blue eyes were bright.

'I believe you're right, too,' he said. 'I'd like nothing better than to get you alone. Just wait until this evening. I can't wait to tell you how much I love you!'

'I shan't be able to sleep this afternoon if you talk like that,' she warned.

He patted her arm. 'Run along now. I have to make my round. Leave the parcel on this desk when you get back. If I'm not here then I'll see you at seven. It will give us a chance for a couple of hours together.'

Her eyes sparkled as he leaned forward and kissed her, and then he opened the door for her and ushered her into the corridor. In that moment Lydia realized that she well and truly loved him. He walked to the stairs with her, and she was reluctant to leave him.

'Go along with you!' he said softly, well pleased with her manner, and she smiled and started up the stairs, her mind already leaping ahead to the coming evening.

On the drive into town, she was lost in thought, and there were many strange emotions vibrant inside her. She had never felt so loving before, and had not suspected that love could make her feel so blithely happy. Now she knew the meaning of love! The knowledge was warm inside her. The future was filled with golden promise and all seemed well.

At that moment a blue Mini shot past her from behind, startling her with its unexpected appearance, and it pulled in front of her and slowed quickly, forcing her to pull in. When she stopped sharply she saw Terry Craig getting out of the car in front, a wide smile on his pale face, and he came back to her, his apparent pleasure filling her with apprehension.

What had she started by talking to him yesterday evening? Had he been the mysterious caller last night on the telephone? Lydia took a sharp breath as she considered, and she knew she had to put an end to this before it really began. Now she had found love with Tim she didn't want complications setting in from any source whatever! She tensed and steeled herself as she wound down her window, and she felt that what she had to say to this strange young man would wipe the smile off his sickly face!

Chapter Six

'Hello there!' Craig greeted cheerily. 'I happened to be passing the Clinic when you came out. Where are you going?'

'Don't you think it was dangerous the way you cut in front of me?' Lydia demanded angrily. 'The road is wet and I might have skidded into the ditch.'

'You weren't travelling very fast, and I just had to stop and talk to you,' he replied, not put out by her anger.

'Well I haven't the time to talk. I'm on an errand, and I have to get back to the Clinic as soon as possible.'

'You said that you were on duty last night!' He ignored her words and leaned an elbow in the window.

'Somebody telephoned me last night, so I learned. Was it you?'

'Of course!' He nodded eagerly. 'I had nothing to do, and I guessed you wouldn't be busy. All nurses ever seem to do at night is sit at their desks and write reports, or read cheap novels.'

'If that's what you think then I must tell you that you're very much mistaken. A night nurse is every bit as busy as anyone on day duty. Now if you'll move yourself I'll get on.'

'You can't be in that much of a hurry,' he contradicted. 'You were driving as if you had all day.'

'I was doing forty! That's quite fast enough for me in these road conditions. You drive much too fast. You're a menace to yourself and every other road user.'

'I know my limitations,' he retorted, smiling. His face seemed finely drawn, and his eyes seemed to indicate that he hadn't slept very well. 'I like to live a bit recklessly now and again.'

'Well don't call me at the Clinic ever again,' Lydia said. 'We're not permitted to receive personal calls.'

'That's nonsense! You just don't want me to ring you. I used to call the other nurses I knew!'

'Perhaps you did, and perhaps they didn't tell you they were warned not to receive personal calls while on duty.'

'All right, so I'm sorry. But look, you needn't be unfriendly with me. I'd like to get to know you better! Can't we meet somewhere when you get off duty?'

'I'm sorry, no! I have a boy friend.'

'But you finished with Doctor Powell!'

'You seem to know quite a lot about what goes on in the Clinic, but evidently your method of acquiring information has let you down in my case. I am now going out with Doctor Fairfax!'

'I've seen you out in his company once or twice lately, but it can't be serious!' His pale eyes looked troubled for a moment. 'I've been watching you for a long time. I'd like to take you out.'

Lydia shook her head. 'I'm flattered by your attention,' she said. 'But it's impossible. Now if you'll move on I'll be on my way.'

'Isn't there anything I can say that will change your mind?'

'Sorry. That's the way it is!' Lydia moved impatiently. 'Look, I am in a frightful hurry!'

'All right!' He was obviously most reluctant to let her go, but he sighed and moved away from the car, and Lydia nodded slowly as she watched his face.

'Thanks!' She put the car in gear. 'Why don't you try to find yourself a nice girl? There are some very nice nurses at the Clinic. You said yourself that you'd been out with Nurse Gerard. What's wrong with her? They don't come any prettier!'

'Looks aren't everything,' he said slowly. 'But it's you I like! Look, I've been very ill and I'm still trying to get over it. You might take pity on me and let me take you out.'

'I couldn't possibly do that,' she said.

He studied her face for a moment, and Lydia felt her patience becoming exhausted.

There was an intent expression on his face, and she wondered what was passing through his mind. But he seemed to read her expression, for he turned away and stalked back to his own car. Lydia watched him through narrowed eyes, and when he had driven on she followed until she reached the town.

She was thoughtful as she went to pick up the parcel. Terry Craig must be haunting the clinic area. Yesterday he had seen her leave, and he had been on the spot again today. Was he spending all his time watching the comings and goings of the nurses?

It was still fairly early by the time she returned to the car with the parcel she had collected, and after locking it in the boot she decided to go for a cup of coffee. But she was afraid of being caught again by Terry Craig. She looked around furtively, half expecting to find his tall figure, but there was no sign of him and she hastened to the restaurant that most of the female staff used when they were in town. She ordered a cup of coffee and sat at a corner table.

Later she returned to the Clinic and deposited the parcel on Tim's desk. Then it was time for lunch, and afterwards she went up to her room to sleep. She found it difficult to slumber, but eventually managed to master her thoughts and slip soundlessly into unconsciousness. When she awoke the time was a little after five.

Sleeping during the afternoon always made Lydia feel sombre when she awakened, and she prepared for the evening with her face and her mind composed. She went to tea, and found little to say to her colleagues at the various tables. It was only when she was back in her room preparing to go out with Tim that she began to break through her reserve, and at seven she went down to find Tim, feeling the lightness of anticipation in her mind and a growing sense of elation.

The evening was fine when they started out, and there was a thin crescent of the moon showing. Tim drove from the Clinic, and Lydia heaved a long sigh of relief as he sent the car along the country road.

'Thanks for picking up that parcel this morning,' Tim commented suddenly. 'I'm sorry I forgot to thank you sooner.'

'That's all right. How are the patients?'

'All pretty much the same, as you can imagine. I expect to be up several times during the night. But we'll discuss this later when you get on duty, Lydia.'

She nodded and settled in her seat. He reached out a gentle hand and took hold of hers, smiling at her as she looked sideways at him.

'I've waited all day for this moment,' he said. 'The hours have seemed to drag.'

'I can't grumble about today because I slept all afternoon,' she responded. 'But I did find the morning rather boring.' She thought of her meeting with Terry Craig, and instinctively looked over her shoulder to see if there were car lights behind, but there was nothing but darkness back there and she faced her front again with relief.

She didn't know what to make of Craig! The fact that he had been very seriously ill did not excuse his bold behaviour, and she hoped he was not going to make a nuisance of himself in future. She didn't know if Tim were a jealous man, but he wouldn't like to know another male was flitting around in the background.

'What are you thinking about?' Tim demanded when she had been silent for quite some time.

'You, mostly,' she replied, and leaned towards him.

'Steady on. You affect me greatly when you get close to me. I'd hate to put the car off the road.'

'Then stop for a bit,' she commanded. 'It's too bad that you have to sneak kisses while we're on duty. When we're away from the Clinic all you do is drive.'

'You don't have to ask me twice!' he retorted gleefully, and slowed the car and pulled on to the verge.

Lydia felt her tension slackening as he

took her into his arms, and she closed her eyes as he kissed her. She had waited a long time for this! The thought was remote in the back of her mind, and she clung to him.

'Lydia, I didn't think I could love you any more,' he said softly. 'But each day finds me more hopelessly entangled with daydreams. Am I being too optimistic, do you think? I waited months for Powell to leave you, and now I can't contain my impatience any longer. I love you, and I want to make progress with that love.'

'I've told you that I think I'm in love with you,' she said cautiously.

'Don't you know for certain?' he prompted.

'I don't know if I know what love is. It would be too easy for me to agree that I love you. The feelings I have for you prompt me to accept them at face value, but it would be dreadful to make a mistake, Tim.'

'I know, my dearest, and I shouldn't be impatient. I'll do my best to control my feelings. You take as much time as you want to make up your mind. But in the meantime you can accept that I love you dearly!'

She looked into his shadowed face and knew he was deadly serious about himself. She believed him! He loved her! But what of her feelings! She searched her mind, scouring into the deepest corners to find evidence. There was a great deal of feeling for him. She knew she was at least infatuated with him. But how did a girl know when true love held her? Could she tell intuitively that any given man was the right one?

'Don't dig so deep, Lydia,' he warned lightly.

'Sorry! I was miles away. But I'm sure I'm in love with you, Tim!'

'I'll settle for that right now,' he retorted, enfolding her in his arms.

Lydia closed her eyes and relaxed. She wanted him to go on holding her until the day she died. She couldn't get enough of his kisses. This had to be love, she thought desperately. No man had ever moved her like this before.

The silence seemed to isolate them, hold them aloof from reality, and there was no other place in the world that Lydia would rather have been at that moment. She was lulled by her emotions, and had never felt so relaxed before in her whole life.

She was suddenly startled by Tim thrusting her away and jerking open the door of the car. Before she was aware of what was happening Tim was gone into the night, and she stared around in complete amazement holding her breath as shock filled her. She didn't move until Tim returned, and he was breathing heavily as he got back into his seat.

'What on earth was all that about?' Lydia demanded. 'Surely I don't affect you like that!'

'I happened to look sideways,' he said thinly. 'There was a face pressed against the rear door window, peering in at us!'

'Surely not!' Lydia was horror-stricken.

'It was no fancy, although I couldn't

believe my eyes at first,' he retorted. 'When I jumped out of the car he was running away.'

'He?'

'Well it wouldn't have been a woman, would it?' He was still breathing hard, and apparently upset by the incident.

'Did you get a look at him?' she demanded.

'Nothing that was good enough to help identify him! I just saw his figure. He wasn't as tall as me, but he could run a lot faster. We'd better move on from here.'

He started the car and they drove on in silence. Lydia was worried, her mind under attack by many dark premonitions. For some reason she thought of Terry Craig, and wondered if he had been prowling around again. He might have been watching the entrance to the Clinic, and he would certainly have recognized Tim's car after seeing her driving it twice. The more she thought about it the more certain she became, but she said nothing to Tim, and when he stopped again later she kept looking around for sign of another car.

'You're jumpy now,' Tim observed after he had taken her into his arms. 'But you needn't worry while you're with me. I'll give a prowler something to think about if I catch him. It's coming to a fine thing when a couple can't park quietly without being disturbed by some idiot!' He thought for a moment, then glanced at Lydia. 'I wonder if it was the same chap who scared Nurse Gerard the other night?'

'I wouldn't like to hazard a guess,' she replied, but she was suddenly cold inside. Had it been Terry Craig on both occasions? She recalled that she'd sensed something strange in his manner, and boldness had been the key factor of his approach to her. She felt a shiver tremor along her spine. She had felt uneasy while he had been talking to her, and yet she hadn't been able to place her fears.

'Well it's time to go back to the Clinic if you're to go on duty,' he retorted. 'These evenings go far too quickly for me. I can hardly wait for your next off day to come round. We're going to London, you know.'

'Did Charles get back today?' she asked.

'Yes. He said nothing about his emergency, so I don't know how it turned out. He'll be on stand-by tomorrow night, so I shall be able to get a good night's sleep for once. But if you have any emergencies tonight it will be me you'll turn out.'

'I'll do my best not to disturb you,' she retorted with a smile.

They went back to the Clinic in near silence, and Lydia found her mind struggling with suspicions and fears. She didn't know what to believe, and dared not broach the subject to Tim. As they left the car and walked through the shadows towards the Clinic she pressed closer to him and looked around fearfully, shivering when she heard a rustling sound in the bushes, but Tim seemed not to fear anything, and she was thankful for his presence as they went on. When they entered the building by way of the side door they almost bumped into Charles Powell and Christine Gerard, and Lydia noticed that Charles gave her a tense stare as they passed. They spoke pleasantly enough to each other, but she was aware that Charles didn't like the sight of her with Tim.

'I hope I don't have to see you before morning,' Tim said with a laugh as they parted at the foot of the front stairs. 'But you'd better hurry if you're going to get into uniform and have supper before going on duty.'

Lydia looked at her watch and nodded. 'I've got enough time,' she said. 'See you later then.'

He nodded, his eyes telling her much more than any words could ever do, and Lydia took his hand for a moment. Then they parted and she went up to her room. There was a tiny feeling of disappointment inside her as she hastily pulled the curtains, then began to change for duty.

When she went down to the dining room

for a pre-duty meal she found Nurse Gerard there, already in uniform and eating her supper. Lydia sat with the girl, smiling as the girl smiled at her.

'You've been quick,' Lydia said. 'I didn't think you were going to make it when I saw you by the side door.'

'Practice makes perfect,' came the steady reply.

'Charles didn't seem too happy. I understand there was something on an emergency for him yesterday. I hope it turned out all right.

'His mother has gone into hospital with cancer. She's not expected to live after the pending operation.'

'Oh!' Lydia was silent for a moment. 'I'm sorry to hear that. It's quite a shock for anyone to get news of that kind.'

'It happened to me over my father about five years ago, and for the same reason,' Christine Gerard said. 'It was a great shock, and sometimes I can still hardly believe that Father is dead.'

'Changing the subject,' Lydia cut in. 'That night you were scared by that prowler outside. Have you heard anything more from the police about it?'

'Nothing. I went to the local station the next day, did you know?'

'No!' Lydia shook her head.

'I looked through some photographs, but I couldn't see anyone even faintly resembling the vague picture of the man who came after me.'

'Did you see anything of his face at all?' Lydia asked, and there was a picture of Terry Craig in her mind.

'No. It was much too dark.'

'Was he a complete stranger to you?'

'I'd never seen him before. I would have known him instantly if I had.'

Lydia thought that ruled out the possibility that the prowler might have been Terry Craig, and she felt relief as she considered it.

'You look worried about something, Sister,' Nurse Gerard observed. 'Is something troubling you?'

'Not really. But I met an old friend of yours yesterday when I was out.'

'Really? Who was that?' The girl frowned as she watched Lydia's face.

'Terry Craig!'

'Him! He was never a friend. He's a head case!'

'What makes you say that?'

'If you knew him at all you'd realize that he's hardly sane. He's been in hospital for a nervous breakdown. He pestered me until I agreed to go out with him, and the first time was also the last. I thought I'd never get out of his Mini alive again!'

'His driving?' Lydia demanded quickly.

'So you've seen him driving, have you, Sister?' The girl looked searchingly at Lydia. 'How did you come to meet him? You didn't let him pick you up, did you?'

'I certainly didn't.' Lydia frowned as she recollected the incidents of the previous afternoon. 'He was watching the Clinic when I drove out.' She went on to explain what had happened, and when she lapsed into silence Nurse Gerard nodded.

'You're lucky you got away from him so easily. But he'll start pestering you now, until you do go out with him.'

'I'm not likely to do that,' Lydia retorted.

'I think he's harmless though. I felt sorry for him, you know. He looked as if he'd had a bad time of it.'

'Could he have been the man who scared you in the grounds the other night?' Lydia watched the girl's face for reaction, but saw nothing beyond a small sign of incredulity.

'No. He wouldn't do a thing like that. From what I learned about him, he's a little bit scared of the dark.'

'Really?'

'Yes! When I was out with Nurse Kent once we met Terry in town, and Nurse Kent started pulling his leg about him coming to see her while she was night duty.'

'But she hasn't been on night duty in months,' Lydia protested.

'That was the point. She thought it would

be funny if he did show up around here while Diana Dillon was on duty.'

'It doesn't sound very funny to me!' Lydia frowned as she shook her head. 'Supposing he had turned up here? Someone would have been badly frightened! Weren't you afraid the other night when you were accosted?'

'Of course, but he knew Kent was only teasing! Don't worry, Sister! Terry Craig is afraid of his own shadow. He said as much when we tried to get him to come here.'

Lydia went on with her supper, her fears laid partially at rest, but she was not happy with what she had learned. Although she said nothing to Nurse Gerard, she could not understand how anyone could have been so foolish as to incite a man to come prowling around the Clinic. The fact that it had happened might well be coincidence, but Lydia was not so certain.

All too soon it was time for them to go on duty, and Lydia felt a kind of relief come to her mind as she took over and let her mind attune itself to routine. Personal thoughts faded away and her worries subsided. But she could feel them nagging in the background of her mind.

Just before midnight, when she sat at the desk bringing her reports up to date, the desk telephone rang shrilly, startling her with its interruption, and she snatched up the receiver with fast beating heart.

'Is that the night Sister?' a rasping voice asked.

'Yes! Who is it that?' Lydia often had calls from relatives of seriously ill patients, and the time of day made no difference to some people.

'You know me,' the voice continued. 'I just had to talk to you!'

Lydia frowned, guessing who it was but unable to recognize the voice over the telephone.

'Is that Terry?' she demanded.

'Right first time, Sister!'

'Didn't I tell you that we're not permitted to receive personal calls while we're on duty?' she demanded, feeling angry. 'Please don't call me here again, and hang up. You may be preventing an important call from coming in!'

She replaced the receiver instantly, and sat breathing deeply, her mind afire with speculation. She felt incensed by his boldness. She had made it quite plain to him that she had no interest in him, but he could not accept that. Then she thought of the incident which had occurred earlier that evening, when Tim had seen a face at the car window, and she wished she had taxed Craig on that. But he was gone now, and she went on with her work, feeling as if she had been subjected to strange pressures without her knowledge of their origin. That was the effect Terry Craig had upon her!

Some of the patients seemed to be particularly troublesome that night, and Lydia hardly found time to rest. The night bells kept ringing, and whenever she looked at the indicator board she saw at least one room number being signalled. When she handed over to Nurse Gerard while she went for her meal she was half afraid to leave the girl in sole charge for fear that she wouldn't be able to cope, but upon her return she was informed that the Clinic had settled down, and the rest of the night was fairly uneventful.

But Lydia found some strange thoughts in her mind. She could not force away the impressions that had come after Terry Craig had telephoned. She was afraid he was going to start pestering her, and she didn't want Tim to find out about it or there would be trouble. But apart from that, she felt certain that Terry Craig had been the man who spied on them when they had parked the night before, and she could not prevent some intuitive sense from repeating that Craig had probably scared Nurse Gerard out in the grounds.

Sleep was the number one priority when Lydia went off duty, and after breakfast she settled down in her room to slumber. It seemed she had hardly closed her eyes when she awakened later, but it was her usual time and she arose immediately and dressed. The afternoon was bright for a change, and she felt her spirits rise as she speculated upon the coming evening.

When she went down for her meal she was stopped in the corridor by one of the duty nurses.

'I was just coming up to see if you were awake, Sister,' the nurse said. 'There's a telephone call for you. Would you care to take it in the office?'

'Any idea who's calling?' Lydia demanded.

'It's a man, although he wouldn't give his name,' came the reply. 'There's no one in the office at the moment.'

'Thank you, Nurse!' Lydia firmed her lips as she walked to the office. She had no doubt as to the identity of the caller. But this time she would be firm with him. She could see a situation building up here, and unless she took steps to stop it she was likely to be overwhelmed. Her thoughts were grim as she took up the telephone receiver.

Chapter Seven

'Hello, Sister,' Terry Craig said as soon as Lydia had given her name.

'I thought I asked you not to call me here.' She spoke sharply.

'But you're not on duty now!' he protested. 'Surely a man can ring a girl at that place. What is it, some kind of prison?'

'I don't want to hear from you!' Lydia said. 'I cannot get interested in you because my thoughts are elsewhere. I can understand your need to make friends with someone, but I'm not the girl, and I shall be most relieved if you would turn your attentions elsewhere.'

'So that's the way the wind blows! I'm sorry to hear that. But can't you meet me this afternoon so we can have a talk?'

'I'm certain that wouldn't help in the

least,' Lydia replied.

'I feel that you're so sympathetic that I need to talk to you. Since I've been ill I have found it difficult to adjust. You're a nurse! You should know how important it is for a patient to be helped even after he's left hospital.'

'I suggest you see your doctor and tell him your problems,' Lydia said, and despite her determination there was sympathy in her voice. 'I'm sorry that I cannot help you, Mr Craig.'

'Please call me Terry,' he implored, and Lydia frowned as she detected a high note in his tones. 'Look, things aren't easy for me! I need an understanding person to hear me out. I have been so depressed lately that I feel like committing suicide!'

'Don't be so ridiculous!' A cold pang stabbed through Lydia, filling her with unreasonable fear. 'You should know better than to talk like that.'

'Then come and talk to me and help me get over this crisis. If you don't you'll surely learn that I'm dead.' He chuckled softly. 'What's an hour of your time compared with the rest of my life? I haven't got a mother to talk to. I need a sympathetic ear, and I took a liking to you as soon as I saw you.'

'But this is ridiculous!' Lydia said sharply. 'I'm sure you must have a number of sympathetic ears to talk to. Didn't your doctor make arrangements for you to get to him when you felt like this?'

'Of course he did! But I'd rather talk to you. You're a nurse. You can't ignore my call for help!'

Lydia compressed her lips, frowning as she considered. She didn't think there would be any harm in confronting him, and it would give her the opportunity to really put him straight. She thought of Tim then, and her heart almost failed her. The obvious thing to do was talk to Tim and tell him all about this business. He would know what to do! But she squashed the idea almost before it was born. She dared not take any risks with her future happiness. Tim might not understand, and he wouldn't like the thought that she had become acquainted with Terry Craig.

'Are you still there?' His voice was filled with sharp query.

'Of course! I'm just thinking!'

'That means you are sympathetic. I knew I had judged you right!' There was triumph in his tones, and for a moment Lydia fought the impulse to replace the receiver. 'Look, I can be at the gate in five minutes. I'm in the phone box in the village. Will you be outside the gate waiting for me?'

'I need to go into the village to do some shopping. Perhaps you would drive me in, and we could talk on the way.'

'That's a good idea. See you in a few minutes.'

'Make it fifteen minutes,' Lydia said, and hung up.

She was thoughtful as she went back up to her room, and she dressed with slow, deliberate movements. Having made the decision to see him, she felt she had done wrong, but she wanted to put him on to another track. There could only be trouble for them if he persisted in his desire for friendship with her.

Fifteen minutes later she was hurrying along the drive to the gate, and she was afraid that Tim might see her and offer her the use of his car, although she would have to make some excuse as it was for running off as she was doing. She sighed heavily when she reached the road and saw Craig's car parked a little way on from the gate, and she looked around furtively before hurrying to it and opening the door.

'Hello!' There didn't seem to be much wrong with Craig as he smiled at her. 'Get in and I'll take you to the village. I didn't think you'd come after all!'

'Why not? You used the right approach! How could any nurse refuse to come after what you said?'

He nodded, and drove on almost before she had settled into the seat. Lydia half turned to face him, and after a few moments he glanced at her, shaking his head.

'Don't stare at me so! It makes me nervous!'

'And you should feel ashamed of yourself, the way you played upon my sympathies. But now I'm here what is it you want to talk about? There's nothing I can do to help you. Surely there must be someone you know to whom you could turn!'

'There's no one. I live with my father. My mother is dead. I don't want to be more than a friend with you. I just need someone sympathetic to talk to at times. Surely that's not asking too much, is it?'

'Well start talking,' Lydia told him. 'We shall be in the village before long, and when I've done my shopping I want to get straight back to the Clinic!'

He glanced sideways at her, and Lydia felt coldness seep into her mind as she saw the strained expression on his intent face. He sighed heavily.

'That's what is wrong with the world

today,' he retorted. 'It's got so that no one has any time for anyone else! You're all too busy to spare a thought for a stranger. A man could be lying in the gutter, dying, for all the care a great number of people would have.'

'Well at least I have stepped out of my own tempo of living to talk to you. I'm one of the few who has stopped to enquire after you.'

'That's right!' He smiled and she noticed how white his teeth were. He was handsome in a fragile way. His features were so fine they looked like a girl's. His blue eyes were the palest she had ever seen, and his fair hair was untidy over his forehead. He looked a lot younger today than she remembered, and she could not help wondering if her first estimate of his age had been too great. Today he seemed like a callow youth who was unsure of himself.

'What was all that nonsense about suicide?' Lydia demanded. 'A person like you is too intelligent to consider such an action. Admit that you only said it to scare me into coming along!'

'I didn't really mean it,' he retorted, 'but don't get the idea that I wouldn't. I first went into hospital because I tried to hang myself!'

Lydia frowned as she studied his intent profile. She could hardly believe her cars, but she sensed that he was serious, and she began to change her mental attitude towards him.

'What was your job before you went into hospital?' she demanded.

'I'm a qualified accountant.'

'That's a very demanding job! I suppose you overworked!'

'That, among other things, caused the trouble,' he admitted.

'And did you try suicide? Was it a serious attempt, I mean?'

'I think it was, although I was probably out of mind. But, you see, my girl killed herself.'

'Your girl!'

'She didn't think I was serious about

marrying her! I kept putting her off while I had my exams and studying to do. She was a few years older than me. But matters came to a head and we quarrelled and parted, and she took an overdose.'

'When was this?'

'At the beginning of the year!' His hands clenched the steering wheel until his knuckles showed white. 'It really threw me. I didn't know what I was doing. My mind became cloudy, and it didn't clear until after I'd been in hospital some weeks. I didn't even know that I'd attempted to take my own life.'

Lydia nodded slowly. 'That was a dreadful period for you,' she agreed. 'No wonder you've been so ill. But you know that no one else can help you, don't you? Didn't your doctor tell you that you have to make the effort to get well?'

'He told me, but it's something that's easier said than done, isn't it? I've made a great fight to get back to my old standard, but just lately I've been losing ground.'

'Why?' Lydia glanced through the windscreen and saw they were approaching the village.

'I thought I was in love with Nurse Gerard, but she lost interest in me!'

'Was it you who scared her in the grounds the other night?'

'Yes!' He inclined his head slowly. 'I was desperate, and I had to talk to her. But she wouldn't listen.'

'Did she know it was you?'

'Not at the time, but I rang her up a few days afterwards and told her.'

'I called the police in that evening. Did you know that?'

'No!'

'Didn't Nurse Gerard tell you?'

'She didn't!' He glanced at Lydia with fear in his pale eyes. 'Did she tell them it was me?'

'No! We've heard nothing more about it. She wouldn't say who it was. But the police told me that there was a similar incident in this village just before you scared Nurse

Gerard. Were you responsible for that, Terry?'

'No! I heard about it, naturally, but it wasn't me. I'm not that kind of a fool.'

'I hope it wasn't you. Would you pull into the park over there? I have to do some shopping!'

He nodded and drove into the car park. Lydia faced him when he switched off the engine. He seemed remote now, and could not meet her gaze He took out the ignition key and began to fiddle with it.

'You seem to be in need of help, Terry,' she said slowly. 'I can't help you though! You really ought to go and see your doctor and tell him the pressures are building up again. He could help you.'

'I'm not going to see him again! I've had enough of doctors and hospitals.'

'Why can't you find yourself a nice girl? That's all you need to help you!'

'My father does his best to keep me away from girls after what happened. I have to promise I won't get serious about anyone.'

'Getting serious about someone would be the best thing that could happen to you,' Lydia said reflectively.

'What about you?' he demanded boldly.

'I'm sorry, but I'm spoken for!' She smiled slowly as she met his gaze

'Doctor Fairfax, I presume!'

'That's right!'

'He didn't waste any time, did he? A week or so ago it was Doctor Powell!'

'No. Doctor Powell never meant anything to me.'

'Then how can Fairfax mean anything? You went around with Powell for months. Surely you didn't just turn from him to Fairfax!'

'No. It's difficult to explain, but I'm certain I can do nothing for you, Terry.'

'I like you a lot,' he said softly, looking into her eyes. 'I don't think I've ever met a more beautiful girl. I've had a picture of a girl like you in my mind for a great many years.'

'What happened between you and Nurse Gerard then? She's a good looking girl!

She's a trained nurse, and very sympathetic.'

'We didn't hit it off. The kind of life I want is too quiet for her.'

Lydia nodded. 'Will you sit here while I do my shopping?' she asked.

'I'd much rather come round with you.'

'But it would complicate my life if we were seen out together,' she explained.

'I see!' He pulled a face. 'All right! I'll wait here for you. But will you let me take you for a drive afterwards?'

'I have to get back to the Clinic!'

'But you're off duty until this evening!' he protested.

'I have to see Doctor Fairfax!'

He sighed heavily and shook his head. Lydia studied him for a moment longer, then got out of the car. She hurried away to do her shopping, and lost herself in what she was doing. It wasn't until she felt a hand upon her arm that she brought herself back to the present, and she turned quickly to see Tim standing at her side.

'Tim!' she gasped in astonishment. 'What on earth are you doing here?'

'I heard that you'd come into the village, and I'm free for a couple of hours. How did you get in? Why didn't you come for the car keys? You didn't walk four miles, did you?'

'I don't like to make a habit of using your car every time I leave the Clinic,' she said.

'Nonsense! Of course you must use it whenever you need it. But how did you get in? There's no bus at this time of the afternoon.'

'I started to walk,' she said slowly, hating herself for having to lie.

'You were going to walk in and back?' He was frowning as he looked into her face. 'Are you crazy, Lydia, at this time of the year?'

'The exercise would do me good, and it was such a bright afternoon.'

'It wouldn't have been so bad had you borrowed the cycle again! But to walk!' He shook his head.

'A boy friend of Nurse Gerard's stopped

164

and offered me a lift,' she went on slowly, watching Tim's face, and she saw a shadow across his features.

'I don't like the sound of that,' he said firmly. 'Hitch-hiking can be a dangerous practice.'

'I wasn't hitch-hiking. I wouldn't have got into a stranger's car. I know the man quite well by sight, having seen him enough times about the Clinic.'

'But supposing a stranger had stopped, and forced you into his car?' Tim demanded.

Lydia shook her head. 'I'm sorry. I won't do it again,' she promised. 'I'll ask to borrow your car in future.'

'That's a good girl.' He spoke in tones that made Lydia feel about six years old, but she could understand his concern, and she felt her heart warm to him. 'But were you really going to walk back? I was expecting you to see me when you awoke this afternoon. I was most surprised when I learned that you'd left the Clinic, walking.'

Lydia didn't know how to answer, so she remained silent. She felt awful having to lie to him, but the situation was not of her making and she was doing her best to keep matters in check and under control.

'Have you finished shopping?' he demanded, and she nodded. 'Good,' he went on. 'My car is in the park over there. Let's go, shall we? Would you like to go for a drive?'

Lydia felt something like panic rise up in her mind as she allowed him to take her arm and lead her towards the car park. It was too late now to tell him about Terry Craig, and her heart seemed to miss a beat when she saw Craig's car standing in the car park almost next to Tim's She froze inside as they entered the park, and she could see Craig in his car. She prayed that he would remain where he was, that he wouldn't make his presence known when he saw her getting into Tim's car, and as they drew even nearer she saw his pale eyes watching her through his windscreen.

But he made no move or gave any sign of knowing her, although Lydia sensed that he was watching her and Tim with the closest interest. She sighed with relief when Tim drove carefully out of the park, and it needed all her willpower to prevent a backward glance at Craig.

'Is everything all right, Lydia?' Tim demanded as they left the village. 'I have the impression that you weren't completely happy at seeing me back there.'

Tim!' She allowed astonishment to stain her features. 'I am always happy at seeing you. It was a surprise, that's all.' She held her breath for a moment as she considered what the scene might have been had she permitted Craig to go around the shops with her. 'I was completely surprised by your appearance, that's all. Why shouldn't I have been happy to see you? I was thinking of getting back to the Clinic in order to see you later.'

'And I've saved you the trouble,' he remarked, smiling. 'I watched you for a few moments before I spoke to you, Lydia.'

'Really?' She smiled, but she was feeling decidedly nervous. 'I had the feeling that hidden eyes were watching me. Did you suspect me of something?'

'Suspect you? Of what?' He raised his eyebrows for a moment, and she saw surprise in his face. 'Good Lord, Lydia! What is there to suspect about you?'

'I might have slipped out to meet another man,' she said steadily, and saw him smile.

'Not you. I suspect there might be a lot of things you might do that wouldn't fit in with your character, but running off with another man behind my back just isn't you.'

'It's nice to know that you trust me to that extent,' she retorted.

'I'd trust you anywhere,' he said fervently.

Lydia thought of Terry Craig and wondered what he was thinking. She was telling herself that a nasty scene could have erupted from that situation, and she realized just how fortunate she had been. She didn't think Tim would accept any kind of an excuse for her being in another man's company, and she vowed then and there that she would not take another chance like that. No matter what Craig threatened, she would never meet him again.

They were silent until they reached town, and Lydia was conscious of a feeling of shock inside her. The way things worked out back in the village, she felt as if she had been reprieved from a terrible fate, and she knew that her hopes for the future would have been dashed had Tim seen her with Terry Craig.

'When's your birthday, Lydia?' Tim suddenly asked. 'It's in June, isn't it?'

'June the tenth, but how did you know?' she replied.

'I wanted to know.' He smiled as he parked the car. 'Well it's my birthday next Friday, and I have a long week-end. I know you're off duty, too, so how about us going to London for the weekend? We could go to my parents for a bit, then go on to your home.'

'That's the nicest thing you've said to me today,' she replied. 'But I don't get off duty until Friday morning, and I have to be back on duty Sunday night.'

'That cuts the week-end a bit,' he mused. 'I don't know if I can get Powell to stand in for me on Friday, so we can get away early in the morning. You could have a nap in the car on the way so we could get on the move early. What do you think?'

'Certainly. It sounds wonderful to me.' Lydia cheered up at his words. 'I can hardly wait for next week. And what can I buy you for your birthday?'

'Buy me?' He sounded surprised. 'Why should you want to buy me anything?'

'Tim! You know you'll look forward to receiving something, surely! I know I'll expect something from you next June!'

'I've already made tentative plans for your next birthday,' he said softly.

'Really?' Her eyes widened as she looked at him. 'That sounds intriguing. Would you care to elaborate on that?'

'Not right now.' He smiled as he shook his head. 'You'll have to contain your impatience. But I assure you that next June will be most vital in your future.'

'Well!' Lydia smiled. 'That sounds significant. I don't know what to make of it.'

'What are we going to do now?' he demanded, turning to her. 'You're looking less strained now, Lydia. Was anything wrong when I first met you?'

'Nothing!' She shook her head. 'I expect I always look a bit strained during the afternoons. It's having been asleep all morning, I expect.'

He smiled and put his arm around her shoulder. 'You're blinking like an owl that's been dragged out into the sunshine,' he observed, and Lydia leaned towards him and pressed her face into his shoulder. 'All those months when you went around with Powell,' he said. 'It seems like a bad dream now. I always had the feeling that you would come to me, Lydia. It's strange how I always clung to that hope.'

She looked up at him. 'Tim, I know you're the only man for me! I can't explain how I know, but it's quite plain.'

'I can see it and you can see it,' he said confidently. 'It is a fact, and nothing else matters.'

He kissed her, and Lydia clung to him for long moments. When he looked down into her face his own features were quite serious, his blue eyes narrowed and keen.

'I dream about you quite a lot, Lydia,' he said severely. 'I don't get any peace – not that I want any from you, mind you.'

'You are always in my thoughts,' she admitted. 'I love you, Tim!'

'Say it again,' he commanded.

'I love you!' She looked steadily into his eyes, and her heart seemed to pound furiously as she saw the expression of love on his face.

'I love you!' He sighed deeply, and a shudder passed through him. 'You're the most wonderful girl in the world.'

'Let's go for a walk before darkness

comes,' she said, smiling. 'We can't sit here all evening telling each other how wonderful we are!'

'Why not?' he smiled broadly, and leaned towards her, kissing her again. 'Why shouldn't we be honest with each other? I love you and I don't care who knows it.'

'All right, so we'll sit here and say nice things to one another!' Lydia leaned back in her seat and watched him closely. He was smiling, and she told herself how much she loved him. It was true that the past seemed like a dream, but now they were together, and the future could only be better than anything either of them had ever known.

But she glanced from the car as he leaned to kiss her again, and she caught sight of a tall, slim figure standing nearby. With a start she realized that it was Terry Craig, and her heart seemed to miss a beat when she realized that he had followed them in from the village and even now was standing by and watching them.

Chapter Eight

When she went on duty that night, Lydia was fearful that Terry Craig would telephone, but midnight came and went and there was no call. She was tense and afraid until she began to accept that it was too late for him to call, and then her mind began to settle down again. When she had the time she sat at her desk in the office and thought about the evening she'd spent with Tim. She'd enjoyed every minute of it, and the knowledge that she loved him was clear and sharp inside. Now she could go over every happy moment, but she found thoughts of Terry Craig intruding, and she became irritated because thoughts of the strange young man were disturbing her peace of mind.

Nurse Gerard came into the office to ask

Lydia to check up on one of the patients, and Lydia asked the girl to sit down for a moment. Nurse Gerard obeyed, looking faintly surprised, and Lydia studied the girl's face for a moment, wondering how best to put into words what was in her mind.

'I told you the other day that I'd met Terry Craig out, didn't I, Nurse?' Lydia began.

'You did, Sister. But he's not the kind of person you'd want to get mixed up with.'

'I have no intention of becoming involved with him.' Lydia smiled slowly, because it seemed to her that she had no choice in the matter. She was becoming involved whether she liked it nor not. 'But what can you tell me about him, Nurse?'

'Not much,' came the instant reply. 'I didn't like him from the start. But I had the devil of a job to get rid of him. He seems to be fascinated by nurses, and if you give him an inch he'll certainly try to take a yard.'

'I met him in the village again this afternoon, and I had a talk with him. I think he still needs treatment from his doctor for that illness he suffered. That's why I wondered what you know about him. He told me he's living with his father, who doesn't want him to have anything to do with girls. Did you ever learn what caused his mental breakdown in the first place?'

'His girlfriend committed suicide, I believe.' Nurse Gerard studied Lydia's face with anxious eyes. 'Don't start showing him any sympathy, Sister, or you'll be pestered by him. He's a very strange boy, and I was a little afraid of him sometimes.'

'He was the man who scared you in the gardens that night, wasn't he?' Lydia demanded.

'Yes!' Nurse Gerard paused for a moment before replying. 'I didn't know it at the time, but when I did learn of it I wouldn't tell the police. I don't think he meant any harm. He was just trying to get to me, but he certainly used the wrong methods.'

'We'll forget about that incident,' Lydia said 'but the police mentioned that a similar incident had occurred in the area just before that night. Do you think it could have been the work of Terry Craig?'

'I wouldn't like to comment on that, Sister. All I know is that I wouldn't go out with him again for all the tea in China! I think he's a head-case!'

'I wouldn't go so far!' Lydia said. 'But do you know where he lives?'

'I've no idea. He told me so many different things. I've come the conclusion that he's a pathological liar!' Nurse Gerard paused and stared seriously at Lydia, then added: 'Among other things! I don't think a girl could be safe in his company, Sister, and none of the nurses will have anything to do with him now.'

'I see.' Lydia could recall her own strange intuitive feelings about Terry Craig, and a frown creased her brow. 'Well we'd better forget about him for now, Nurse. Who is the patient you wish me to see?'

'Mrs Andrews! She's complaining that she can't sleep, and she's already had her sleeping tablets.'

'All right. I'll go and attend to her shortly. Will you make a round of the top floor now? I'll start my own round in about five minutes.'

Nurse Gerard nodded and departed, and Lydia sat for a moment thinking of Terry Craig. She was undecided what to do. If she had known the name of Craig's doctor she might have rung him and warned him that Craig was showing signs of abnormality. But she knew she couldn't interfere, and she was worried and thoughtful as she went about her duties.

Making her round, she went in to check each patient, deliberately restraining her thoughts as she went through her routine. She found some of the patients awake, and did what she could to make them comfortable. There was always a number of patients who could not sleep despite the drugs that were administered, and Lydia always tried everything she knew to help them.

When she met Nurse Gerard again she sent the girl to get her usual cup of tea, afterwards intending to get her own. She did another round of the two floors while the girl was away, and when she came to an empty room she paused to shut the door, which stood ajar. Going on to the end of the corridor, she returned a few moments later to find the door ajar again, and she paused while a sense of fear spread swiftly through her.

With her hand held out to grasp the doorknob again, Lydia paused while her intuition sent a spasm of speculation through her mind. Some intangible sense seemed to warn her that all was not as it should be, and she hesitated in the act of closing the door once again.

Was there someone in the room? She felt ice in her breast as she considered, and she was afraid to push the door wide while her mind grappled with her fears. Then she thought of Terry Craig, and her pent up breath left her with a rush. Surely he hadn't entered the Clinic!

Lydia took a deep breath. Her heart was pounding and there was a constriction in her throat that threatened to choke her. She tensed and pushed the door wide, suddenly and without warning, and her eyes narrowed as she stared into the dim interior of the room. She couldn't see anything suspicious. There was an unmade bed and a bedside cabinet, but the light switch was behind the door and that part of the room was in deeper shadow. She looked through the crack in the door, and felt a wave of horror assail her as she caught a slight movement through the crack. She heard the unmistakable sound of clothing rustling, and for a moment her heart seemed to stop beating and a flood of nameless fear chased through her mind.

Very quickly she reached out and pulled the door to, closing it firmly. Then she turned away and walked quickly to the head of the stairs, watching the door of the room over her shoulder, and she saw the doorknob turn slowly and the door opened a fraction again.

Lydia felt stifled as she reached the top of the stairs. She was terribly afraid, but she wasn't running in panic because there was someone in that room, some intruder who had no right to be there. She knew it would be foolhardy to tackle anyone without help, and she hurried down the stairs and went into her own office, telephoning the night porter and asking him to come immediately to her office. When she mentioned there was an intruder she heard a gasp at the other end of the line, then silence, and she replaced the receiver and waited in a fever of impatience and fear for the porter to arrive.

'What's all the trouble, Sister?' The porter, Dave Arnold, a burly man in his middle forties, appeared in the doorway armed with a heavy torch and a short, thick stick. His face was gaunt, and Lydia felt sorry that she'd had to awaken him.

She quickly explained her experience, and saw disbelief come into his expression.

'I assure you I haven't been dreaming, Dave,' she said.

'I'll believe you, where I wouldn't believe some of the others, Sister,' he said. 'Which room is it?'

'I'll show you,' she said steadily.

He nodded and led the way out of the office and up and she paused when she pointed out the door of the room, which was ajar again. Arnold nodded and motioned her to step aside. He went forward, taking a firm grip on his torch and the stick, and he didn't pause when he reached the door, throwing it wide open with a heavy shoulder against the centre panel.

Lydia heard the door open so far that it thumped heavily against the wall, and she knew there was no one standing behind it now. But Dave Arnold went into the room and pulled the door forward, switching on the light and walking into the centre of the room as Lydia moved to the doorway. She didn't need him to tell her that the room was deserted. She could sense it, as clearly as she had sensed that someone had been in it only a few minutes before.

'Imagination, Sister?' the porter demanded, a tight little smile on his lips.

'No, Dave!' She was conscious that her tones were trembling. She explained again what she had seen and sensed, and they looked around the room together.

The window was not fastened. It was closed but the sneck was out of place. The porter locked the window then, the catch squeaking a little as he pushed it home. Then he ran his hand along the window sill, and when he looked at it there were tiny pieces of mud adhering to his fingers.

'Mud,' he said needlessly, holding out his hand for Lydia to inspect. 'And it's still wet. Now how would mud get on that sill? These rooms are kept spotlessly clean, aren't they?'

Lydia nodded, her breath trapped in her throat. She moved across to look at the floor behind the door, where she knew the intruder had been standing, and her keen brown eyes saw mud and dampness on the floor.

'Look at this,' she said sharply. 'Now do you believe me?'

The porter joined her and stared down at the floor, nodding his head slowly the while, and then he looked into Lydia's eyes, his face serious.

'You'll have to report this to the police,' he said thinly. 'They'll come and investigate. They'll be able to tell if anyone had used the fire escape outside.'

Lydia nodded, and some of her fear left her now she was certain there had been an intruder. She thought she knew the identity of the unknown man, but her thoughts were centred upon what she would tell the police when they asked her for a statement. She would have to mention Terry Craig, and that might mean word of her meeting with Craig getting to Tim's ears. But this was too serious a matter to be hushed up, and Lydia sighed heavily as she led the way back to the office.

'I'll go back to my room,' Dave Arnold told her. 'I don't suppose the police will want to question me. I can't tell them anything. But you'll know where I am if I should be needed.'

Lydia nodded and sat down behind the desk. As the porter departed Nurse Gerard appeared in the doorway, and the girl was frowning as she entered the office.

'Something wrong, Sister?' she demanded.

'Listen,' Lydia said, and called the local police station. She watched Nurse Gerard's face as she spoke to the policeman who answered, and fear showed plainly among the other expressions which crossed the girl's face as she grasped the import of what Lydia was saying.

The police agreed to send someone along, and Lydia replaced the receiver and faced her subordinate.

'Did you actually see the man?' Nurse Gerard demanded.

'I saw a movement in the room, certainly,' Lydia replied.

'Weren't you scared?'

'Terribly, but I managed to keep it under control.' Lydia realized that she was trembling now and she clenched her hands convulsively. 'I don't think there's any danger now, Nurse. He will be a long way from here now.'

'Do you think it was Terry Craig?' Nurse Gerard demanded.

Lydia took a deep breath and held it for a moment. Then she shook her head slowly.

'I don't know, Nurse.'

'Are you going to tell the police about him?'

'I don't know.'

'It will be foolish not to. If he isn't guilty then he'll have nothing to worry about. If he is guilty then he ought to be stopped before he goes too far.'

'Didn't you say that you had encouraged him to come into the Clinic by night?'

'That was some time ago, and he must have forgotten that by now.'

'Well we can't have him prowling around

the place, if it was him!' Lydia reached a decision. 'I shall have to tell the police all I know, and that includes about the incident involving you.'

'Oh Lord! That detective with the Bogart manner will be after me for not reporting it to him. I said I'd let him know if I remembered anything else.'

Lydia got to her feet. 'You'd better get back to duty, Nurse,' she said. 'I'm going for my tea. I shan't be long, and keep an eye open for the police. We don't want a lot of noise at this time of the morning.'

'I'll come for you if they arrive before you return,' Nurse Gerard said.

Lydia departed, and she had to steel herself as she walked along the corridor to the dining room. Everywhere was silent and still, and her nerves were playing her tricks in protest at the shock which she had received. But she was convinced that the intruder had been Terry Craig, and the knowledge lessened some of her horror.

She had barely finished her tea when

Nurse Gerard appeared to tell her there was a policeman in the office waiting for her, and Lydia tried to steady herself as she followed the nurse back to the office. She sent Nurse Gerard on about her duty before entering the office, then went in swiftly before her nerves could react further against the situation.

A tall, powerfully built man in a raincoat turned to look at her, and Lydia was surprised to see that he did resemble a film star who had made a name for himself acting in tough roles. But he spoke pleasantly enough, and they both sat down. Lydia gave him her statement, recalling every detail of the incident that had scared her. The detective made copious notes, and remained silent except for an odd question or two. Lydia told him everything she knew about Terry Craig, including the way he had telephoned her and how he had been the man who scared Nurse Gerard. She even mentioned that Nurse Gerard had dared Craig to enter the grounds of the Clinic at night. When she finished her statement the detective nodded.

'I know of this man Terry Craig,' he said sharply. 'I wouldn't have thought he was your type, Sister!'

'I'm certainly not interested in him,' she replied. 'He threatened to kill himself if I didn't meet him, and you can imagine what effect that kind of threat had upon me.'

'I understand, Sister. Well I'll go and have a word with Terry Craig, and if he's the man then we'll have to do something about him. Did you know there's been two other incidents involving women in this area since your Nurse Gerard was frightened in the grounds here?'

'I didn't know!' Lydia was shocked by the news.

'Well it's a fact.' He got to his feet and put away his notebook. 'You should be very careful about your contacts away from this place. I wouldn't advise you to see Craig alone again until I've cleared him or arrested him.'

'Arrested him?' Lydia felt a coldness begin to seep into her mind. 'You won't make a charge against him for what happened tonight, will you?'

'He broke the law by coming on to these premises! But if he came only to see you, and lost his nerve at the last moment to declare himself, then I'm sure we won't press charges, but I'm more interested in these other cases. They're far more serious.'

He took his leave, and Lydia went with him to the entrance. She was worried after he had gone, and she could not settle in the office with her reports. She made another round of the Clinic, and even went into the operating theatre to look around. But there was nothing to alarm her, and she finally went back to the office and settled down to work.

Before going off duty next morning, Lydia made Nurse Gerard promise not to talk about the incident that had occurred, and the girl was plainly disappointed at having the morsel taken from her, but she grudgingly agreed that it would be better to remain silent, and Lydia went to see the porter before going off duty. Dave Arnold agreed to say nothing, although he couldn't understand why nothing should be said.

'Surely Matron should be told,' he protested.

'If anything comes of it from the police then of course she will be told, but it could be bad for the nerves of all the nurses to know there's someone prowling around.'

'I get you, Sister. All right, my lips are sealed.' He grinned at her. 'But I shall be taking a look around the grounds after dark from time to time in the future, and if I lay my hands on anyone who has no business on the place then he'll be sorry for a very long time afterwards.'

Lydia went to breakfast and then to bed, and she slept soundly until the early afternoon, but as soon as she opened her eyes all the fears and the problems of the previous night returned to her mind, and she lay for some time trying to work out if it had really happened or if she had dreamed about it.

When she went down to the dining hall for her meal she found Nurse Gerard already there, and the girl seemed bursting with news. Lydia took her food to the same table and sat opposite the girl.

'What's happened?' she demanded.

'That detective was back here this morning. He saw Matron, and she wants to see you as soon as your presence can be arranged. I said this morning that you should have reported to her about that intruder.'

'I suppose it's all over the Clinic now, is it?' Lydia demanded.

'Of course, and everyone is going to be afraid to go out after dark.'

'That was what I was trying to avoid,' Lydia said, and forced herself to eat her meal.

'I wish I knew what the police are doing about Terry Craig,' Nurse Gerard went on. 'Do you think they'll arrest him?'

'It all depends on what he's done,' Lydia replied wisely, and she escaped from the dining room as quickly as possible.

Going along to Matron's office, she tapped sharply at the door, and stiffened herself when she heard Matron's voice declaring the door was unlocked. Realizing that she might have to explain her own motives in not submitting a report on the incident, she walked into the office expecting to be on the carpet, but Mrs Tate greeted her cordially, and invited her to sit down.

'Sister, you were very brave last night, and you kept your head. Your actions must have averted what might have been an ugly incident. I'm glad you did the right thing. Were you so very frightened at the time?'

'Terrified,' Lydia admitted. 'I suppose it did happen! It wasn't just a dream, was it?'

'The police have ascertained that someone did enter that room last night. The deposits of mud prove it, and there are some fingerprints on the window sill and the glass. The fire escape ladder leading to the ground also showed signs that someone had used it within the last twenty-four hours. They have a suspect, and I understand you know him. Is this the reason why you didn't report this matter to me?'

'I thought it might be someone I know, and that his presence on the premises was the result of some stupid intention to play a joke on me, Matron.'

'I see. I presume you're talking of this man Terry Craig, whom the police are questioning. Can you be sure it was he?'

'Not absolutely, Matron, but I have a good idea it was the man, although the thought didn't come to me until afterwards.'

'I see. Well in future you'd better put everything into your report, Sister. I'm not rebuking you because if this man is a friend of yours and he was intent upon playing a joke upon you then obviously the affair needn't be blown into oversize and out of all proportion.'

'I didn't say he was a friend of mine,

Matron,' Lydia said quickly.

'Very well, Sister. I'll say no more about it, but please remember about the future. I expect the police will keep you informed of their progress in the matter, and they may want to question you again. That will be all.'

Lydia thanked the matron and departed, relieved that the matter hadn't developed more seriously. She was on her way back to her room when Tim appeared in the corridor, and she felt a sinking sensation around her heart as she went towards him. His face told her nothing at a distance, but when she reached him her searching eyes discovered that he was in a serious mood, and she wondered how much he had learned about Terry Craig.

'Lydia, are you all right?' he demanded in tones which expressed his deep concern.

'Yes; why do you ask?' she countered.

'All the stories I heard today about that incident last night made me think that perhaps you'd suffered a terrible shock and might not get over it,' he retorted. 'What really happened?'

She told him, avoiding the fact that she had met Craig outside the Clinic.

'I think he took Nurse Gerard's words seriously about sneaking into the Clinic one night,' she ended. 'That's all there is to it, Tim.'

She heard him sigh sharply, and watched his face anxiously as he placed a heavy hand upon her shoulder. 'You'll have to go around as soon as you get on duty in future, checking that all windows are fastened, and it might be as well to keep all unoccupied rooms locked.'

'I don't think it will happen again,' she said quickly. 'No harm was done.'

'I hope the police are not jumping to conclusions as you are doing,' he said seriously.

'What do you mean?'

'It may not have been the man you think it was. I think you should treat the whole matter as if you knew it wasn't this man Craig. Only then will you have the right attitude of mind to combat the situation.

Promise me you won't treat it lightly, Lydia.'

'I promise,' she said instantly, struck by his seriousness. 'I haven't been treating it lightly, Tim. I was badly scared last night, and I think my nerves will be affected by what happened for a long time to come.'

'Well I'm glad that you had the sense to act as you did. There is no telling what might have happened had you decided to tackle the man singlehanded. I shudder to think of what might have ensued, Lydia.'

She nodded, her eyes bright with speculation. She felt again a pang of the suffocating fear which she had experienced the moment she realized there was someone behind the door of the room, and she clenched her hands as she fought down her panic. But she was relieved that Tim hadn't heard about her knowing Terry Craig, and she hoped that part of it would remain unknown to him.

They made arrangements to meet that evening, and as the hours passed, bringing Lydia even closer to the moment when she had to go back on duty, she found her nerves reacting unfavourably towards the situation, but she steeled herself for the ordeal and went on duty to face reality.

The waiting for more news from the police was worse than anything she had ever experienced before. She could not accept that Craig was the man responsible for the attacks upon local girls, and she kept thinking of the closeness of her own escape from a similar incident. She had the feeling that perhaps she ought to see Terry Craig again, if only for her own peace of mind, although she knew such an action would be the height of folly.

Time seemed to stand still, as if to punish her for the way she had been forced to be disloyal to Tim by Terry Craig's trickery to see her alone. But she was safely out of his grip now, she told herself. She wouldn't meet Terry Craig alone ever again, no matter what inducement he used. Nothing would ever be permitted to step between Lydia and her love for Tim.

Chapter Nine

A sense of anti-climax gripped Lydia as the following days passed by. It was only the thought that she and Tim were going to London for the week-end that sustained her in the nerve-racking wait for news. But when Thursday night came and she went on duty she fought her mind to overcome the doubts and the fears that lurked within. The next morning she would be leaving the Clinic for three days, and what might lay in the future after that she neither knew nor cared.

She hadn't left the Clinic since that day Craig had blackmailed her into seeing him, and she knew she wouldn't go out again alone for the rest of the time that she spent there. She was not afraid of Terry Craig! Rather she had a kind of presentiment that it would be much better for her to stay well away from him.

After taking over her duties she made the first round of the night, checking the patients and noting those who would most likely require her attention before morning. She checked the lists that had been left for her and satisfied herself that the windows and doors of the empty rooms were securely fastened. When she returned to the office to sit down and work on her reports she heaved a long sigh, and could not help wishing that Friday morning had already arrived.

The next instant the telephone rang, and she froze as she automatically lifted a hand to take up the receiver. The instrument kept shrilling insistently, and she found that her mouth and throat were dry as she hesitated. Then she steeled herself mentally and took up the receiver, forcing her voice to sound natural as she spoke.

'Pinewood Clinic!'

'Sister Redmond! Why did you set the

police on me?'

She firmed her lips. It was Terry Craig. She drew a sharp breath as she considered, and was tempted to hang up instantly, but that action wouldn't solve anything, and she knew it.

'Is that Terry Craig?' she demanded, although she recognized his tones.

'Who else?' he demanded. 'I thought you were a friend of mine. You didn't seem like the other nurses. They were laughing at my expense, but you seemed more mature and sympathetic.'

'It was you here in the Clinic the other night,' Lydia said. 'Don't deny it. You broke the law by coming in like that, and I had no choice but to telephone the police.'

'I won't deny it to you. It was me. But I didn't admit it to the police, and they don't have any evidence against me.'

'What did you want here?' she demanded fiercely. 'I suppose you know you gave me the fright of my life, and it was a good thing for you that you'd gone before the night porter arrived.'

'I only wanted to talk to you. I was in need of help. You could have helped me considerably. I was only asking for a few moments of your time.'

'If you need help then you should see your doctor. He's more qualified than I to help under all circumstances.'

'He can't help me at all. I get so frustrated, and all I want is to talk to you. May I see you tomorrow?'

'I'm sorry, but I won't be here at all this week-end. I'm going home to see my parents in London?'

'When are you leaving?'

'First thing in the morning, and I shan't be back until Sunday.'

'Can I see you in London?' he asked eagerly. 'I'd like to take a trip, and I could drive you. That would save your fare.'

'I have a seat in a car going to London,' Lydia said. 'I'm sorry, Terry, but there's nothing I can do to help you. Why don't you follow my suggestion and see your doctor?

You can explain all your problems to him.'

'I don't want to see the doctor!' He almost shouted, and Lydia winced as she took the receiver from her ear. 'Why can't you understand that I need you?'

'I must ask you to hang up,' she said, cutting across his anger. 'This is a busy line, and there may be important calls waiting to come in.'

'I thought your kind of person always did what she could to help people! I need help. I've got to talk to someone or I shall go mad.'

'What did the police have to say to you? Did they question you about other incidents?'

'What other incidents?' He pounced like a big cat scenting prey.

'In a case like this the police usually ask questions about all similar cases they have on hand, don't they?' she countered.

'I don't know anything about any other cases! What do you take me for?'

'It came out that you scared Nurse Gerard

here in the grounds. The police take a dim view of that sort of thing, and no doubt you were warned to stay well away from Pinewood, weren't you?'

'I wasn't doing any harm,' he protested. 'You've got me all wrong. When can I see you? What about Monday afternoon?'

'I'm sorry, Terry, but I don't think it would be wise for us to meet again.'

The line went dead immediately, and Lydia frowned as she replaced the receiver. She sighed heavily as she considered. There had been a note of hysteria in his voice that she didn't like, and she knew that he was moving into some kind of a mental crisis. She wished now that she had done something about Craig's doctor, and for a moment she wondered what she could do. Then she firmed her lips and lifted the receiver again, calling the local police station and asking for the detective who had visited her previously. She had to wait a few moments, and in that time she tried to decide what to say.

'This is Detective-sergeant Swinfield! What's the trouble, Sister Redmond?'

'Sergeant, Terry Craig has just called me again.'

'Was he offensive in any way?'

'Oh no! Quite the opposite, in fact! I'm worried about him. He sounds as if he needs help. I expect you know his history better than I! I'm afraid that if he doesn't get help he might go out and do something dreadful. It has been known to happen in such cases.'

'I think I know what you mean, Sister, and I have taken steps to have him watched. Of course we can't be behind him every minute of the day.'

'I was thinking that perhaps we could do something more constructive,' she retorted. 'If you know who his doctor is it might help to have a word with him, get him to call on Craig. He'll be able to see that the boy is under pressure. Failing that, a visit to Craig's father might produce results. But something should be done about him.'

'All right, Sister. Leave it to me. I appreciate your concern, and thanks for taking the trouble to let me know. I'll see what I can do. Let me know if Craig does try to contact you again.'

'I'm going to London this week-end, so I shan't be around until Sunday evening.'

'Good. That will give us a clear field where you're concerned. But I have got a watch on the Clinic. It's not full-time, you understand, but there is a man in the area.'

'Thank you, Sergeant. Goodnight!' Lydia hung up with a sigh of relief escaping her. She sat for a moment considering her actions, and was conscious that she was pleased with what she had done. She thought of Craig for some minutes, and knew that he needed further hospital treatment. She hoped her action would start a process which would help him recover completely from the mental troubles which bothered him.

As she made her later rounds she could not help wondering if Craig had come to the

Clinic again, but she was secure in the knowledge that all windows and doors were locked. She had the relief of knowing that it had been Craig before, and she didn't think his mental condition was such that he might contemplate violence against anyone. But one could never be too careful in a situation like that, and from time to time she did find herself looking anxiously over her shoulder as she walked the long corridors.

The night seemed to pass more slowly than usual, no doubt because she was filled with anticipation for the morrow. But the patients who were usually troublesome seemed even more difficult, and her patience was taxed to the limit as she did what she could for them. Then came the dawn, and soon it was time to go off duty.

She had breakfast with Nurse Gerard, and before the meal was over Tim appeared, smiling at her and raising his eyebrows in an unspoken question. He came and sat down at her side as Lydia finished the last of her coffee.

'I'm all ready to go,' he said cheerfully. 'But I'm not going to rush you. I can see that you have to change. What time shall we meet?'

Lydia stifled a yawn as she consulted her watch. Tim saw her action, and hastened to say.

'Look, you must be really tired. Why don't you take a couple of hours now and sleep? We can start off later.'

'That would be a waste of perfectly good time,' she retorted. 'I can sleep as easily in the car as in my bed. It will be a four hour drive to London in the least, and if I sleep all the way I shall be quite refreshed by the time we get there.'

'Just as you wish.' He smiled, and was light hearted and filled with anticipation. His high spirits made him boyishly cheerful, and Lydia studied him intently, happy with his appearance.

'I'll be ready in thirty minutes,' she said. 'I must take a shower and pack an overnight bag.'

'And we'll go to my parents for today, and go on to your home tomorrow afternoon until Sunday,' he said. 'Have you made the arrangements with your mother?'

'I called her yesterday,' Lydia said. 'Everything is arranged.'

'Then I'll get back to my room and finish my preparations,' he said. 'See you in the hall in thirty minutes.' He glanced at his watch to check the time, and they both got up together and departed, going their separate ways in the corridor.

Lydia was feeling on top of the world as she took a shower, then dressed for the trip. It didn't take her long to pack a bag, and she was ready within the thirty minutes he had stipulated. A sense of great elation touched her soul as she went down to the hall, and when she saw Tim standing there in wait she paused and looked at him with a great softness in her brown eyes. He looked up and saw her, and a smile came to his face. She saw love in his expression, and knew this was the most wonderful moment of her life. Going down to join him, she was aware that even the drab morning seemed brighter than was possible.

'All ready?' he demanded tenderly, and took her case and held her elbow as they walked to the door.

The sun was shining as they walked across to the car, and Lydia felt as if a heavy weight had suddenly lifted from her mind. She paused as Tim unlocked the car, and when she took a deep breath she tingled inside and felt as if she would not be able to contain all the wondrous emotions becoming animated in her mind.

'Now you get into the back and stretch out on the seat,' Tim commanded. 'I'm not a bad driver so you should have a smooth run, and you ought to be able to sleep all the way to London.'

Lydia nodded and blinked her eyes. She was feeling very tired, and when she got into the back Tim stuck his head into the car and arranged the cushions there for her.

'You're looking after me like a mother hen

chasing around a prize chick,' Lydia told him, and saw him smile.

'Well you're certainly a prize chick, although I don't think your mother hen description fits me! But make yourself comfortable and close your eyes. We have a long drive ahead of us.'

'What's our route?' she demanded, settling down.

'Oh, Norwich, Ipswich, Colchester and so on. But you needn't worry your head about that. Are you quite comfortable?'

'Fine thanks!' She reached out and put her arms around his neck; pulling him towards her, and they kissed gently. When he disengaged himself he was smiling, and she watched him as he slammed the door and went around to the driver's seat.

As they started off Lydia lay back and closed her eyes. But Tim remonstrated with her.

'You're not going to rest like that,' he said sharply. 'Lie on the seat and sleep properly.'

She smiled and sighed, stretching out and

making her head comfortable on a cushion. She found she couldn't keep her eyes open any longer, and as soon as they closed she drifted into a deep and satisfying sleep...

When she awoke, Lydia opened her eyes and lay staring up at the interior of the car while she tried to recollect her scattered wits. Then she turned her head and looked at Tim's back, her eyes softening as she watched him. She sighed and stretched, feeling much refreshed, and he heard her and glanced quickly over his shoulder.

'Hello, Sweetheart, so you're back with me again. How are you feeling now?'

'Fine thank you!' Lydia sat up and leaned forward to place her face against his. She kissed the side of his neck, and he lifted a hand and touched her cheek. 'Where are we?'

'We've just passed through Chelmsford. You've had over three hours sleep. But we won't have a busy day today. We'll save our running about for tomorrow.'

'When you think of stopping I'll come and

sit in the front with you,' she told him.

'We've still got some way to go, so I suggest we stop for something to eat. I told my mother I'd be home well after lunch, so we'd better have a break now.'

Lydia nodded, and kept her face close to his for a moment, but eventually he sighed regretfully and leaned forward a little.

'I like that,' he said, 'but it's affecting my driving.'

He glanced in the rear view mirror and Lydia caught his eye. She saw he was smiling, and she leaned forward again and kissed the back of his neck.

'I'd better stop the car and let you get in front with me,' he remarked. 'There's a lay-by just ahead.'

They stopped and Lydia got out of the car to stretch her legs. Tim joined her and they walked to the end of the lay-by and back before going on. Lydia talked generally until Tim turned off the road and parked behind a roadside cafe.

'I've stopped at this place before,' he said

as they got out of the car. 'The food is quite good. But we want just a snack because Mother will have food waiting for us when we arrive.'

'I had an uncle who lived at Wimbledon. He was killed in the war, but Aunt Betty still lives there.'

'You were born during the war, weren't you? That makes you pretty old.' He spoke in teasing tones, and Lydia clutched at his arm.

'I expect you were, too,' she countered.

'Only just! I'm thirty-one now.'

'And I'm twenty-seven.'

'A beautiful twenty-seven!'

'Flatterer!' She entered the cafe in front of him and he selected a corner table and held her chair for her before going to the counter for sandwiches.

'Tea or coffee?' he called to her.

'Coffee please!' She watched him, standing tall and straight, his handsome face alive with interest, and she felt a growing emotion inside that seemed to fill her with intolerable pressure.

They loved one another! The knowledge put a sparkle into her brown eyes. She breathed deeply and felt a tingle travel through her. Many times she had tried to wonder what love was like, but she had never imagined it could do such things to a girl as she was now experiencing. Despite the tiredness still gripping her she felt light hearted and gay, jubilant in a subdued way. She was agog with happiness, and the future promise of it all filled her with impatience. She wanted to know now what lay in store for her, and her heart began to pound as she mustered her feelings and concentrated upon the thought that she was in love.

They didn't stay long in the cafe, and when they were driving on once more Lydia put her head against his shoulder. He sat very still, concentrating upon his driving and she watched his profile intently, drinking in his appearance.

'What are you thinking now?' he asked without looking at her. He was staring ahead, watching the other traffic.

'I was just telling myself how much I love you, Tim,' she said very seriously.

'Are you sure?'

'Sure of my love?' She nodded slowly. 'I'm positive.'

'What makes you so sure?'

'I don't know. It's just something I know. I don't even have to think about it.'

'Are you getting serious about me?'

She smiled as he glanced at her, and she made no reply.

'That's a bit disappointing,' he went on. 'Suddenly lost your tongue, or shouldn't I have asked the question yet?'

'I was just considering it. I suppose I am getting serious. I am in love with you, and I know there'll never be anyone else for me.'

'Is that a fact?' He glanced at her again, and there was a smile on his face. 'Well I feel exactly the same way about you, only I've known longer than you have. I'm in love with you, Lydia, and nothing will ever change it. I've been in love with your image for as long as I can remember, and the moment I first met you I knew you were the girl of my dreams.'

'That's a very nice thing to tell a girl,' she said slowly 'Have you ever said that to another girl, Tim?'

'No.' He shook his head. 'This is the first time, and I really mean it.'

'It's strange how we came together after I went around with Charles all those months.'

'You were never in love with him,' he said sharply. 'I used to watch you very closely. I could tell you and he were never more than mere friends.'

'That's true.' She nodded slowly. 'But it wasn't just because Charles isn't the serious type. I couldn't get close to him, and I didn't want to.'

'I understand.' Tim smiled at her, holding her gaze for a moment. Then he shook his head and returned his attention to the road. 'We'd better finish this conversation or we'll be off the road. You take away my concentration Lydia, and that's bad.'

She smiled as she stared ahead through the windscreen. She knew what he meant, and she knew that he understood her completely.

Later he stirred in his seat and glanced at her. They had stopped at some traffic lights, and while they were waiting to go on he reached out and touched her hand.

'Not far to go now,' he commented. 'I'm sure you'll get on very well with my parents. When I spoke to them about you over the phone the other night they were enthusiastic. My mother feels it is time I settled down, so don't be surprised if she eyes you speculatively.'

'I shan't mind that in the least,' Lydia said eagerly. 'But what are your views on marriage?'

'I'll tell you all about them one day,' he said in secretive tones, and with that Lydia had to be content.

Chapter Ten

Shortly after they turned into a quiet street and parked before a large detached house. Tim switched off the engine and turned to her with a smile on his face.

'We're here,' he said needlessly. 'Home sweet home! I hope you'll like it.'

Lydia nodded as they got out of the car, and she took her case from his hand when he removed it from the boot. As they walked up the short path to the house the front door was opened, and Lydia found herself face to face with a small, attractive woman whose face showed a remarkable resemblance to Tim's. She was smiling, and her blue eyes were as pale as Tim's.

'You've arrived at last, Tim!' she greeted breathlessly. 'I've been watching for you for the last hour.'

'We stopped at a cafe for something to eat rather than make the run without a break, Mother,' he declared, 'I want you to meet Lydia Redmond. I told you all about her the other evening.'

'Hello, Lydia. You're very welcome. I had given up hope that Tim would ever bring a girl home.'

'I'm pleased to meet you, Mrs Fairfax,' Lydia replied, grasping the woman's hand. She looked into the pale blue eyes and thought they belonged to Tim. 'Tim is very like you,' she said.

'Everyone tells me that!' Mrs Fairfax was pleased. 'But come in and make yourself at home. You must be tired after your trip.'

'She was on night duty last night, and had only three hours sleep this morning,' Tim said, shaking his head. 'We could have waited until she'd had her rest, but we wanted to make the week-end as long as possible.'

'Then you must have a rest this afternoon, Lydia,' Mrs Fairfax said.

'I shall be all right until tonight,' Lydia said. 'But if I start yawning later please don't think it's because I'm bored.'

They entered the house, and Lydia was escorted into a very large lounge. She sat down and Tim joined her.

'Mother's gone to make a cup of tea,' he said. 'She'll fuss around you, Lydia, so be warned. All her life she wanted a daughter in the family, but all she got was me! What about you? I've heard you talk of your parents, but have you any brothers or sisters?'

'None. I'm an only child myself. I would have liked a brother or a sister, I think.'

'You won't need one now,' he retorted, taking her hands. 'I'm very happy to see you here in my home, Lydia, and I hope you'll come again a great many times.'

She looked into his eyes, her face showing her joy, and he smiled slowly as he gathered her into his arms and then kissed her soundly.

'I used to detest the long drive down here

from Norfolk,' he said. 'In future we must arrange all our off-duty times to correspond.'

'That's all you want me for,' she said teasingly. 'My company on the long trips.'

'I want your company all the time,' he retorted, kissing her again, and Lydia hugged him for a moment.

When Mrs Fairfax came back into the room again, with a tray and tea, Lydia was feeling flushed with happiness. Getting away from the Clinic had removed an invisible weight from her mind, and she could realize now, miles away from the scene, that the Clinic had been getting her down despite the fact that her mind was fully occupied with thoughts of Tim.

'I have prepared lunch for you,' Mrs Fairfax said. 'Molly is serving it in the dining room now.'

'Mother is a good cook,' Tim said, grinning at Lydia. 'So you need have no fear of being poisoned.'

Lydia smiled. She could tell that Mrs

Fairfax was well accustomed to Tim's teasing, and she also noticed that the woman was studying her very closely.

'I'll leave you two to eat in peace,' Mrs Fairfax said when the maid appeared to tell them the meal was ready. 'Father will be home soon, I expect. He's got to go out tonight, but he said he wanted to see you before he went.'

'Did I tell you that Father is a free-lance journalist?' Tim asked Lydia as he ushered her along to the dining room.'

'You didn't,' she replied. 'It sounds an exciting occupation.'

'I would have followed in his footsteps if I hadn't got this bee in my bonnet about being a doctor,' he continued. They went into the dining room and sat down at the table, and a rather middle-aged woman appeared to serve them with their meal. 'Hello, Molly,' Tim greeted her cheerfully. 'This is Lydia Redmond, the most important girl in my life.'

There was pride in his tones, Lydia noted,

and she was pleased.

'I'm very pleased to meet you, Miss,' the maid said cheerfully. 'It's about time Tim brought home a girl.'

'That's exactly what Mother said!' Tim chuckled throatily, and Lydia watched him in fascination. He seemed so unlike the man she knew at the Clinic, and yet she liked this side of him better than the professional man that he was on duty. 'I wouldn't be surprised if you and Mother had got together to discuss my life, Molly. I know Mother has been dying to get me married off.'

'A man has to settle down some time, Tim,' came the keen reply. 'Even doctors get married.'

Lydia wisely said nothing, and they began their meal on a high note of happiness. Afterwards, Tim took her back into the lounge, and a tall, very much older image of Tim got to his feet and put aside a newspaper to come forward to meet her.

'My father!' Tim said cheerily. 'Mind how you shake hands with him, Lydia. All that holding of a pen has given him a grip like a bear.'

'I'm very pleased to meet you, young lady,' Mr Fairfax said. 'I've been wondering what kind of a girl it was that had gained our Tim's interest. Now I've met you I don't have to wonder any longer. I thought Tim had gone blind, truth to tell, but he's restored my confidence in him. I hope you'll have a pleasant week-end with us. I shall be darting away shortly, but in my business I don't work orthodox hours. I have to work when I can catch up with the people I need to talk to. But I shall be seeing you again before the week-end is over.'

Lydia liked Tim's father from the outset. He seemed a cheerful, kindly man, and there was deep understanding in his blue eyes. She could see where Tim got his good looks and his pleasant manner from, and this meeting with Tim's parents made her feel all the more certain that she and Tim were meant for each other.

'I'll show you up to your room now,

Lydia,' Tim said, 'If you want to have a nap this afternoon then you can do so. But your ordeal of meeting parents is over. I've got mine to come.'

'My parents won't eat you,' she said with a laugh.

'You've been keeping them pretty quiet,' Tim retorted, smiling.

'Well you'll have the chance to meet them tomorrow, and then you can decide for yourself what they're like.'

'It may be too late for me then,' he said, chuckling.

'What does your father do?' Mr Fairfax asked. 'Has he an interesting occupation? I always like to know about people. That is my job. I have to write a fair number of articles each month on people and their ways of life. Perhaps I'll find some copy in your father.'

'He's a dental surgeon,' Lydia said. 'I doubt if his occupation will interest you, but he writes articles, and scripts for boys' picture books in his spare time.'

228

'Does he now?' Mr Fairfax's blue eyes gleamed. 'That is interesting. I think I shall have to pay him a visit. Perhaps you will make an appointment for me to see him when you go home tomorrow.'

'Gladly.' Lydia smiled. 'When will it be convenient for you?'

'I can always fit in an appointment,' came the eager reply. 'You tell him I can call at any time which will suit him.'

'You'll get used to this,' Tim said with a grin. 'I have to keep my eyes open for unusual people. Father will have you doing the same thing now.'

'It's all grist to the mill,' Mr Fairfax said. He had a winning smile, and Lydia was quite taken up by his engaging manner.

'It isn't fair that you should get other people to do some of your donkey work,' Mrs Fairfax said. 'Show Lydia up to her room now, Tim, and let her get some rest. She looks worn out. You ought to have more thought for her, dragging her out so soon after coming off night duty.'

'It was her idea,' Tim said instantly. 'Although I must admit that it appealed to me.'

He took Lydia's hand and led her from the room, and in the hall he put his arms around her. She looked up into his face and felt her emotions stirring.

'My darling,' he said huskily. 'I love you so much. I wish we had got together when you first arrived at the Clinic. I've had to wait eight months to get close to you!'

'Better late than never!' she retorted. 'Don't look back into the past, Tim. It's over and done with.'

He nodded, and turned away to pick up her case, and he took her into his arms once more. He kissed her before continuing. 'You do look very tired still, Lydia. Why don't you have a nap until tea time?'

'What will you do?' she asked.

'Probably sit talking to Mother. Father will be going out shortly. I've never known him not to have someone to see. But you need a sleep, and I insist that you lie down now. You'll be all the fresher for this evening.'

'What plans have you made to that end?' she asked.

'I'll let you find out when the time comes,' he replied. 'Now I'll leave you and let you get some sleep.'

Lydia was feeling rather tired, and she made no protest, after he had kissed her, when he moved to the door.

'If you sleep too long I shall come and call you,' he warned. 'But you need another two or three hours.'

Lydia mentally agreed, and she heaved a long sigh when he departed. She sat down on the foot of the bed and realized that the idea of sleep had never seemed so inviting. She removed her outer clothes and lay down, drawing an eiderdown over her, and before she knew it she had fallen asleep. She knew no more until she opened her eyes to find grey twilight filling the room.

At first she could not place her surroundings, and it wasn't until her thoughts started moving again that she recalled everything. Then she sat up and looked around, getting off the bed to go to the window. She looked out into the shadowed garden, and a great square of light lay across the bedraggled lawn, issuing from the kitchen windows. Rain pattered against the window panes, and she shivered and turned away, switching on the light before drawing the curtains.

By the time she had dressed there were footsteps on the stairs, and a moment later a gentle hand tapped at the door. Lydia went to open it, and found Tim standing there. He smiled when he saw her.

'I didn't wake you up, did I?' he demanded gently.

'No. I've been awake some minutes.'

'You're looking better, anyway!' He took her into his arms and held her close for a moment without kissing her. 'I can see sleep in your eyes. You're beautiful, Lydia! I've never met a more perfect girl.'

'They do say that love is blind,' she said

wisely, and saw him grin.

'Well I've got good eyesight,' he retorted. 'Come on, come and have some tea, and then I'm going to take you out to see the bright lights. Back at the Clinic there's nowhere a man can take a girl for a good night out, but here in London it's different.'

'I am quite impatient to know what you call a good night out,' she said as they descended the stairs.

'You'll find out this evening,' he retorted.

When they entered the sitting room Mrs Fairfax nodded when she looked at Lydia.

'You're looking much better now, Lydia,' the woman declared. 'It was too bad of Tim to bring you away this morning without letting you have your sleep.'

'All's fair in love and war,' Tim quoted. He pulled out a newspaper from a rack and opened it to the entertainments page. 'I'm thinking of taking Lydia to a show this evening. Can you suggest anything, Mother?'

'Did Lydia come prepared for such a

treat?' Mrs Fairfax asked. 'Surely she didn't put her best dress in that case she brought with her.'

Tim looked at Lydia, his eyes filled with a questioning light.

'Have I boobed, Lydia?' he demanded.

'I didn't bring much in the way of a change of clothes,' she said, smiling faintly. 'But I expect I can make myself look presentable enough for you.'

'Then take her to dinner at the Rendezvous Restaurant,' Mrs Fairfax said. 'Afterwards you can go to any one of a number of shows and have a nice time.'

'Do you like films, Lydia?' Tim demanded.

'I haven't been for a long time, but I used to see a lot of films in my teens. I like anything serious, but I can't stand the sort of films they're making these days.'

'That doesn't sound too hopeful,' he said with a smile. 'But we can sort it out after tea.'

'Which should be ready now,' Mrs Fairfax

said, getting to her feet. 'If you'll excuse me I'll go and help Molly lay the table.'

'May I help, Mrs Fairfax?' Lydia demanded.

'No, my dear! You're not going to do a thing in this house over the week-end. You take it easy.'

Tim smiled as his mother left the room. 'Mother is going to spoil you, I fear,' he remarked. 'But you've always been a busy sort of girl, Lydia. I think you can do with some spoiling.'

She smiled at him, and he crossed to her side and sat down, taking her hands. She felt drawn closer to him than ever before, and she knew it was because of the atmosphere of his own home. She could glimpse another side to him, here in the privacy of his family, and she liked the impressions she was getting. She hoped he would be similarly impressed by her home, and she gave a little thought to her parents as she considered. Tim kissed her lightly on her cheek, and when she looked up at him he smiled.

'A penny for them, Lydia!'

'I was just thinking of tomorrow, when I get you at my home!'

'That sounds ominous!' He stroked her cheek, and let his breath escape in a long, slow sigh. 'I'm pleased I brought you here today. It's nice to get you in different surroundings. The Clinic makes you seem a little unreal and inhuman. I mean that nicely, by the way. But here, in the familiar setting of my home, I can appreciate the kind of girl you are.'

'My thoughts were running along those lines! It's strange how we very often seem to be thinking the same thing.'

'Great minds think alike! Or minds in love do!' He kissed her, and held her hands tightly.

Lydia had never felt happier. The pleasant atmosphere that surrounded them grew in intensity during their tea, and afterwards, when she went up to her room to change, she had the strange feeling that she was walking on air. Her spirits were high, and her face, when she looked critically at it in the mirror, was flushed and stained with happiness. Her high colour surprised her, and her sparkling eyes seemed to belong to a stranger. While she sat considering, her pulses raced and her heart pounded.

This was love, she told herself slowly. Nothing short of it could affect a girl like this! Her hands were trembling and there was a tightness in her throat. Even her thoughts were affected by her feelings. She sensed that everything about her had become coloured by what was happening to her. Life seemed warm and rosy. Her attitudes had changed completely.

When she was ready to go out she went back down to the sitting room, and Tim uttered an ejaculation at the sight of her.

'Well you look good enough to take to Buckingham Palace,' he declared. 'I'm glad I've put on my best suit.'

Lydia was studying him, thinking how handsome he looked in his pale blue suit. His face was shining, and when she stood nearer to him she caught the gentle tang of after-shave on his face. Mrs Fairfax came into the room a moment later and beamed at Lydia.

'You're looking a picture, Lydia,' she said. 'I hope you'll enjoy yourself tonight.'

'I'll see that she does,' Tim promised. 'But now we'd better be on our way. See you later, Mother!'

'Have a nice time!' Mrs Fairfax replied...

Lydia found the evening exceeding her expectations. They went to see a film instead of waiting to see a show, and afterwards Tim took her to a large restaurant where they had a wonderful meal. It made a complete change for Lydia, who was accustomed only to the small pleasures of night life in a small Norfolk country town, and the only disappointing thing about the whole evening was the speed with which time passed. When they were at last on their way home she sighed happily and wished they could experience the whole time all over again.

'Tired?' Tim demanded as they entered the house. The time was almost midnight, and there was just the hall light burning.

'A little,' she admitted. 'But it's been a wonderful evening. Thank you for showing me such a great time, Tim!'

'This was only the start,' he said cheerfully, leading the way into the sitting room and switching on a reading lamp. The dull glow gave the large room a sense of intimacy which matched Lydia's mood, and she pushed herself into Tim's arms and closed her eyes as he kissed her. 'Just wait,' he promised. 'If you call this living then I've still got a thing or two to show you.'

'I can't wait to find out,' she told him.

He kissed her passionately, and Lydia felt her senses receding as she clung to him. She was vibrant with emotion. Her whole being cried out to him for more. She had never been so moved in her whole life, and she subconsciously realized that her whole outlook was changing imperceptibly. Before she began going with him her life had revolved around nursing. Nothing else had mattered except duty. Now everything was slipping into prearranged places, and her priorities had changed a great deal.

'Would you like some supper?' he demanded softly.

'No thank you! I think I've eaten too much already.'

'A cup of hot milk then?'

'Nothing at all, thank you.'

'You're ready for bed. I can see that. Don't let me keep you up any longer, sweetheart. It's been a long day for you.'

'An important one,' she said.

'Has it really?' He kissed her.

'Most important. I wish I could relive it!'

'That's the nicest thing anyone has ever said to me.' He smiled at her. 'But tomorrow will be my great day. I have to meet your parents.'

'It won't be an ordeal for you, will it?' She was suddenly concerned for him.

'An ordeal?' He shook his head. 'It will be the greatest pleasure in the world.'

'I'm so happy, Tim!' She pressed her face against his for a moment, and he held her tightly, forcing all mundane thoughts from her mind with his nearness.

'Now you'd better go to bed,' he said firmly. 'See you in the morning, Lydia.'

She kissed him on the mouth and clung to him for a moment longer, then smiled and reluctantly turned away. She went up to her room and prepared to go to bed, and there wasn't a single unharmonious thought in her mind. Her sleep that night was sound and sweet.

Next morning when she awoke, Lydia found the same rosy attitude persisting, and when Mrs Fairfax suggested that Lydia go shopping with her while Tim talked with his father, Lydia jumped at the idea. The sun was shining when they set out, and Lydia listened intently to all that Mrs Fairfax had to say. She wanted to learn as much as possible about Tim's life as a boy, wanted to get all the background information available.

They went for coffee later, and Lydia found herself getting over her first strangeness with this woman who had mothered the man she loved. Mrs Fairfax soon became silent, encouraging Lydia to talk about herself, and Lydia found she could talk quite easily to this attractive woman. She told her all about life at Pinewood, and talked about her hopes for the future.

'I can see that you and Tim are serious about one another,' Mrs Fairfax said. 'I'm sure you're both very well suited, and it is about time Tim thought of settling down. Don't get the idea that I'm in a hurry to do some match-making, Lydia, but Tim needs to settle down. I'd like to see him leave Pinewood now and come nearer home. He could go into general practice in this district, but he won't even consider it until his personal life has been decided.'

'I expect Tim would like to get back to London, anyway,' Lydia said thoughtfully. 'There's nothing much out there in the wilds of Norfolk.'

'Would you come back this way if Tim did?' Mrs Fairfax watched Lydia with steady eyes.

'I'd go where ever Tim wanted me to, with no hesitation or reservation,' Lydia said promptly.

'But would you like to make the move?' Mrs Fairfax persisted.

'I think so.' Lydia narrowed her eyes as she thought of Pinewood and the area in which it was situated. She didn't think she would want to go back into a general hospital, but there were Clinics and Nursing Homes around London where she could easily obtain a position, and that part of her life no longer worried her.

'Well it has been most pleasant to have you with us, Lydia,' Mrs Fairfax said, cutting in across Lydia's thoughts. 'I hope you will come again, and often. Tim was never one to bring home a girl, and both his father and I have been waiting impatiently for the most important girl in his life to turn up. Having met you, I can understand why Tim is so keen on you, and I do hope everything will work out the way that is indicated. But I suppose we'd better get back to the house now. It will soon be time for lunch, and then you're going on to your parents.'

'I wish our stay with you could have been longer this time,' Lydia said as they prepared to leave the restaurant. 'But Tim is intent upon meeting my parents, and I know they're just as keen to meet him.'

'That's all right, my dear!' Mrs Fairfax leaned forward and patted Lydia's hand. 'There will be other times, and I'm sure that we are going to be close friends in the future.'

Lydia agreed with that. Already she seemed to be looking upon this vivacious woman as a second mother, and she didn't even pause to wonder about the apparent ease with which this state of affairs came about. Everything to do with Tim seemed to follow naturally and fit into a pleasant pattern. When she did think about it she could hardly believe that in so few weeks this situation could have settled itself so completely. Yet there had been no signs of haste on Tim's part or her own.

It was just another indication that something more than mere chance was taking a hand in their lives, and Lydia relished the thought and cherished it in her loving heart!

Chapter Eleven

When they were driving to Shepperton after lunch, Lydia felt her anticipation rising. Tim hadn't been the type to take many girlfriends home, and she hadn't been the sort of girl to take home any boy that she had known. She had never been that serious over anyone, and now the man she loved was with her and about to meet her parents. She glanced at Tim, smiling as she took in his features.

'Did you feel yesterday anything at all like I feel today?' she asked him quietly, and he glanced at her and smiled.

'It was a bit nerve racking,' he admitted, 'but it was worth, it. Don't let it worry you, sweetheart. I'm not going to take violent exception to your parents, and I don't expect them to turn round to you and say that they find me totally unsuitable for you.'

'They wouldn't presume to sit in judgement on any friend of mine,' Lydia said. 'But it isn't so much the thought of taking you home for the first time as taking you home at all. I never made a habit of it, Tim.'

'Well my parents told you the same thing about me. That proves we're two of a kind. What more do you want to accept the fact that we were meant for each other?'

Lydia smiled as she regarded him. She could only agree with what he said. She was now completely in love with him and she didn't care who knew it.

When they reached her road she began to tense a little, and Tim smiled at her with complete assurance. She pointed out the drive that gave access to her parents' home, and he turned into it and drove over protesting gravel to the house set back from the road and screened by leafless trees. When Tim brought the car to a halt before the house he sat for a moment in silent contemplation, and Lydia watched his face for reaction.

'Were you born here?' he demanded at length.

'Yes,' She nodded. 'Father's family always had a lot of money, and we've lived here for many years.' She reached out and touched his hand. 'Come on, let's go inside and get it over with.'

'I think you're more nervous than I am,' Tim observed. He leaned towards her and kissed her lightly on the lips. 'No wonder you never brought home many of your friends if you got this nervous at the thought of it.'

She smiled and they got out of the car. Tim took their cases and Lydia led the way to the house. As she opened the front door her mother appeared from the lounge, and Lydia hurried forward and threw herself into her mother's arms, kissing her cheek and hugging her tightly.

'Mother, I'm so pleased to see you!' Lydia cried, and caught her breath as she turned to introduce Tim, who came forward with a carefree smile on his face, putting down the cases and extending his hand.

'How do you do, Mrs Redmond?' he said lightly. 'I'm very pleased to meet you. Lydia hasn't told me much about her parents. I was afraid there was something of a shock awaiting me when I arrived here, but I can see that I have nothing to worry about. I wondered where Lydia got her beauty from, and now I know.'

'Hello, Tim,' Mrs Redmond said. She was tall and slim, with brown eyes very much like Lydia's, and with a few grey streaks in her dark hair. 'Please come in and make yourself at home. This is quite an event for us. I've waited for this moment for a very long time.'

'That's near enough what my mother said when I took Lydia in,' Tim said, and he crossed the threshold and closed the door.

'Where's Father?' Lydia demanded.

'He's at work in his study, but he left orders that you were to take Tim in to meet him as soon as you arrived. I'll get some tea while you're talking to Father, so come into the lounge afterwards.'

Lydia took Tim's hand and led him along the hall, and they paused outside the study for a moment.

'All right?' she demanded, and Tim pulled a face.

'What are you trying to do?' he demanded lightly, 'scare me?'

She laughed and tapped at the door, opening it quickly when a deep voice called out an invitation to enter. She walked in ahead of Tim, and her eyes lit up when she saw her father, who threw down his pen and got to his feet instantly, coming around the desk set by the window and holding his arms open to Lydia, who ran to him and hurried into his embrace.

'Father, it seems such a long time since I saw you last.' She kissed his cheek and then drew away from him, looking towards Tim, who was standing just over the threshold, a smile on his face. 'I want you to meet Tim,

Father, Doctor Tim Fairfax, to give him his proper title. Tim, this is my father!'

Tim came forward with outstretched hand, and Lydia saw that he and her father were about the same height. William Redmond shook hands warmly, and eyed Tim keenly.

'Very pleased to meet you,' Tim said.

'It's my great pleasure,' Lydia's father replied. 'I hope we shall see more of Lydia now she's found someone who lives in London. Perhaps you'll see that she comes home more often, Tim!'

'I'll certainly do that,' Tim said, nodding.

'It's too far to come for an ordinary day off,' Lydia protested, 'and I don't have a car. Before Tim and I started going around together I didn't have much chance of getting a lift home.'

'Well you won't be able to use that excuse any longer,' her father said. 'Eh, Tim?'

'She won't,' Tim said confidently. 'We'll be home every other week end, if we can arrange our off-duty hours satisfactorily.'

'That sounds more like it,' her father said. 'Well are you going to sit down or have you something else to do?'

'We don't want to disturb you longer than necessary, Father,' Lydia said quickly. 'Are you busy?'

'I'm always busy, as you well know,' William Redmond said with a smile. 'But I can always make time for my daughter.'

'Tim's father is a free-lance journalist, Father, and when I happened to mention that you did some writing on the side he was most interested, and he'd like to meet you and have a chat about your literary efforts.'

'Very well,' came the instant reply. 'Let me have his telephone number and I'll give him a tinkle. Your home is at Wimbledon, I believe, Tim?'

'That's right. It's not too far from here.' Tim smiled. 'Father travels miles to get his stories. I'm sure he'll find you interesting.'

'I'll call him, I promise you.'

'What are you writing now, Father?' Lydia asked.

'I'm still working on picture stories. I find them quite easy to do, and I like them. I don't suppose they're sufficiently adult for you, Tim, but you can look at some of them later.'

'They're the war stories in pictures, are they?' Tim demanded. 'I have read some. They're quite good in their class.'

'I know they're not high class.' William Redmond smiled. 'But I get tremendous excitement and satisfaction writing them. It makes quite a change from pulling teeth.' He glanced at Lydia. 'It's about time I had another look at your mouth, my girl.'

'That's the worst of having a dental surgeon for a father.' Lydia said to Tim. 'I must have the most well kept set of teeth in the country.'

'They're most important to health,' Tim said. 'I agree with your father there, Lydia.'

'Oh, don't get me wrong! I agree with him,' she retorted. 'And I can see that you two are going to get along very well. Already you're ganging up on me.'

She was happy though, and later, when they sat down to tea, she could tell that Tim had made himself at home. He seemed like a well established visitor to the house, and she could see that he had made a good impression upon her parents. She was filled with relief. This was the most important phase in her friendship with Tim, and they both seemed to have scrambled over their respective hurdles with great accomplishment.

They stayed in the house that evening, sitting in the lounge and chatting, and Lydia learned some more about Tim as she listened to his pleasant voice. Later her father went into his study, to return some moments later with a chess set.

'Do you play, Tim?' he asked eagerly.

'I was some sort of a schoolboy champion,' Tim declared. 'But it is a long time since I had a game.'

'Well thank goodness for that,' Lydia said cheerfully. 'I always get roped in for a few games when I come home. I'll make sure I always bring you in future, Tim, and you'll be able to keep Father happy and save me from that dreadful fate of playing chess.'

'You don't like the game?' Tim demanded.

'It isn't that so much as getting beaten every time I play,' Lydia retorted.

'I like to meet players better than myself,' Tim retorted. 'One can always learn something then.'

'That's an admirable attitude to take, Tim,' William Redmond said. 'But I'm nowhere near champion class, so I expect we'll have a real tussle.'

Lydia sat talking to her mother while the men played, and she was in a high form of elation as she relaxed and forgot completely about the situation that existed at Pinewood. This week-end was really just what the doctor ordered, and she knew that the following weeks would be coloured by these events.

By the end of the evening her father had won two games and Tim had taken the other four. Lydia was happy for her father's sake, because he worked too hard and too long and never found enough relaxation. Tim was happy, and his blue eyes told her so whenever she happened to glance at him. While they were having supper he sat by her side, and reached for her hand under the table.

Lydia was sorry that the day had come to an end, and after supper they sat chatting again.

'When are you leaving tomorrow?' her mother asked.

'In the morning, I'm afraid,' Lydia replied. 'I'm on duty tomorrow night, and I shall have to get some sleep before then. But we'll be home again in a week or two.'

'I hope so,' Tim declared. 'I've never spent a better week-end. If we never do any more than this any weekend, I shall be happy.'

Lydia nodded, filled with pleasure by his words. The week-end had been a milestone in her own life, and she would always be able to look back upon it without difficulty and with the fondest memories.

Later, when she went to bed and the house became silent and still, she lay thinking about her past and wondering about her future. How she had managed to live fairly happily before meeting Tim she would never know. He was everything to her now, and she knew it without reservation. When she thought of all the times she had gone out with Charles Powell, when she might have been with Tim, she shuddered, for it had been such a waste. Thinking back now, she could realize that Tim had exerted some kind of influence over her before they'd got together. She had always been aware of his presence around the Clinic.

Drifting into sleep, she awakened next morning with disappointment inside her. They were going back today! It was the first time she had ever felt disinclined to return to Norfolk! But Tim was going with her, and they'd be together at the Clinic, but it wouldn't be the same as staying in London with nothing to distract them from each other.

It was raining, she discovered, and the grey skies were glowering and weeping as if to mourn the fact that the happiest week-end of her life was at an end. But she consoled herself with the fact that there would be other week-ends, and she dressed and prepared for their return.

Tim was already up and ready when she went down the stairs, and he took Lydia into his arms in the privacy of the lounge, kissing her tenderly and looking intently into her face as he held her close.

'You look as reluctant to go back as I feel,' he commented. 'Have you enjoyed this week-end, Lydia?'

'More than I could ever tell you, Tim. I'm already looking forward to the next time.'

'It will be as soon as we can make it,' he said firmly. 'I love you, Lydia! I knew that before the week-end started, but now I feel it more intensely. You're the only girl I shall ever want. My hopes for the future have never been higher. I keep telling myself how fortunate I am that you never took to

Charles Powell. I love you so much that it would have been a crime against Romance itself if we'd never come together.'

She stroked his face and pressed her cheek against his. 'I love you, Tim,' she replied earnestly. 'I know you love me because what you've just described is exactly the way I feel about you.'

He sighed heavily. 'We'd better start back fairly early this morning, my love. You've got to sleep this afternoon, and I don't want to have to drive too fast in that weather out there.'

She nodded. 'We'll leave soon after breakfast,' she agreed. 'But I don't like the thought of going on duty at the Clinic tonight. You've spoiled me in some way, Tim. Once I lived for nothing but my vocation, but now there's you, and I've pushed my duty into the background and made it second in importance.'

'I feel the same way about you,' he replied. 'We're going to have to come to terms with our feelings, Lydia, but time is new yet, and when we settle down to the fact that we're in love then everything will assume its correct perspective.'

She nodded, but she was thoughtful, and at breakfast she said little while Tim chatted with her parents. All too soon it was time for them to take their leave, and Lydia was truly regretful that the week-end was at an end.

'Don't forget to ring Tim's father,' she said to her father as they walked out to the car. The rain had eased considerably, and somewhere up among the murky clouds the sun was shedding a little brightness in its feeble efforts to get through to the earth. But the wind howled through the trees and gusted about them spitefully.

'I'll call him this morning,' William Redmond promised. 'Be careful on the roads, Tim. It's a treacherous day.'

'I'm always a very careful driver,' Tim replied, nodding. 'I was a casualty officer at a hospital for several months without a break, and I'll never forget some of the cases that came to me as a result of road accidents.'

Lydia kissed her mother tenderly, promising to come home again as soon as possible, and Tim shook hands with her father, and Mrs Redmond hugged him impulsively before he got into the car. They departed then, and Lydia turned to wave for as long as she could see her parents. But once out on the road, she faced her front with a sigh and stared through the windscreen, her mind dwelling upon the past two days.

'I've never known a week-end to go so quickly,' Tim remarked slowly. 'But you've always had that effect upon time, Lydia. Ever since I've known you I've been aware of the fact that evenings and days just seem to fly past when you're around. At this rate we're both going to be very old before we know where we are.'

She smiled, and leaned towards him, resting her head against his shoulder.

'Are you sad?' he continued. 'You look it.'

'I am. I wish we had another week together.'

'So do I! But it isn't too bad, you know. At least we are together at the Clinic.'

She nodded absently, and they settled down to the long drive. The weather wasn't too bad, and they made good time, but it was the middle of the afternoon before they reached Pinewood, and Lydia was stiffly tired when they got out of the car. Rain was pattering down through the surrounding trees, and everywhere looked dreary and sad. She felt a lump rising in her throat as she took her case from Tim, and they entered the Clinic and paused at the foot of the stairs.

'You'd better get some sleep now, Lydia,' Tim said. 'We shan't be able to meet this evening. By the time you've had your rest it will be time for duty.'

'You're on call from six, aren't you?' she asked.

'Yes, Sweetheart!' He smiled as he nodded. 'I'll come and spend some time with you once you get on duty. I'll let Powell know we're back, in case he wants to get out for the evening. But you run along and get some sleep.' He put a hand on her arm for a moment. 'Thanks for making my week-end so wonderful,' he said softly. 'I've never enjoyed myself more. That's the truth, Lydia. I hope all our week-ends could be as happy as this one's been.'

'We can make them so,' she said eagerly, 'even if we can't get to London.'

'That's the spirit,' He nodded his agreement, and looked around quickly before kissing her.

Lydia went slowly up to her room, and she sighed heavily as the clinical atmosphere of Pinewood assailed her once more. She had been home for a week-end many times in the time she'd been here, but she had never felt so reluctant to come back as she felt now. In her room she unpacked her case and put her clothes away, letting her mind wander back over the events of the past days. Then she tried to compose her mind to reality, and she drew her curtains and settled down to sleep.

It was dark when she awoke, and for some moments she lay in a dreamy state, not really asleep and not properly awake. Her thoughts were idle, her mind almost blank, and she sighed once or twice as she slowly came back to full awareness. The darkness of the room was overwhelming, and she pushed aside the bedclothes and arose, fumbling across to the light switch and depressing it, flooding the room with stark light, and when she glanced at her watch she knew she had overslept and would have to hurry in order to be ready for duty at the appointed time.

Slipping on a dressing gown, Lydia went along to the bathroom for a shower, and afterwards put on her uniform and prepared herself for duty. She went down to the dining room for her meal, and was relieved to see Nurse Gerard there, all ready for duty.

'Hello, Sister!' There was pleasure in the girl's tones as she greeted Lydia. 'Did you have a nice week-end?'

'Fine, thanks, Nurse,' Lydia replied. 'It was so good that I didn't feel like coming back.'

'Well it's a good job you were away, because we had some excitement that you've done well to miss.' Nurse Gerard's tones were filled with vibrant emotion. 'Friday night was like a scene from a horror film.'

'What happened?' A frown touched Lydia's face. Her mind delved into the possibilities that the girl's words conjured up, but she had no idea what was coming. However Nurse Gerard's first words brought home the sharp reality.

'Terry Craig was here during the night! I was on duty and he came out of an empty room and grabbed me. Fortunately I didn't scream, or I'm sure he would have done something to me. He was looking for you, Sister, and he said a lot of strange things. I really thought he was going to harm me, and he made some threats against you.'

'Terry Craig!' Lydia frowned as the import

of what was said got through to her mind. 'What did the police have to say this time?'

'The police!' Nurse Gerard shook her head. 'I didn't tell anyone about this! I'm sure Craig would have come back here again and got me if I said anything. But I've got to tell you because I had to let him know you'd he back on duty again tonight, and that is the only reason he left quietly. I've been on tenterhooks all week-end, and I was half inclined to ring your home and tell you not to come back. But I didn't want to make trouble for anyone, because I didn't report what happened Friday night.'

'You did the wrong thing,' Lydia said sharply. 'I think you should have reported the matter to the police. After the warning Craig got the first time he came here they would have been able to do something about him this time. It isn't right that he should get away with it.'

'He's in a bad way mentally, Sister,' Nurse Gerard warned. 'You'd better be careful how you handle him if he shows up here again. When he learned that you'd gone to London for the week-end with Doctor Fairfax he said some dreadful things.'

'Well I'm not going to take any chances,' Lydia said firmly. 'If Craig knows I'm back on duty tonight he'll certainly make some attempt to contact me again, and if he is coming here then I want some protection. If the police catch him red-handed then they'll be able to do something about him. I'm going to call them in right away!'s

Chapter Twelve

Lydia was aware of the drama in her voice as she spoke, and she saw surprise in Nurse Gerard's face, but she was emphatic, certain that she could not afford to take any chances with Terry Craig. She had already informed the police that Craig was in a poor mental condition which was deteriorating still more, and she felt that something had to be done to stop him getting into an even worse state.

She finished her meal quickly, hardly aware of what she ate, and then she went along to the office, taking over from Sister Eaton well before her appointed time. In answer to her colleague's query, she merely said:

'I've got a telephone call to make, Emily. You run along now, I'll handle it from here.'

When she was alone in the office she called the local police station and asked for Sergeant Swinfield! She was informed that the sergeant was off duty, but when she mentioned Terry Craig's name she learned that the Sergeant would be informed and that she could expect a call from him.

Waiting in the office seemed to tax her nerves to their limit, and Lydia thought of her happy week-end and felt bitter that she had to come back to this situation. When the telephone shrilled she started nervously, and paused for a moment before lifting the receiver, fearing that it might be Craig himself calling. Then she took a grip upon herself and lifted the receiver, giving her name in sharp, clipped tones.

'Sister Redmond this is Sergeant Swinfield. What's the trouble?'

Lydia suppressed her relief and told him what she had learned from Nurse Gerard about the incidents of Friday night. When she finished the sergeant became very business-like.

'In response to your earlier call about Craig, Sister, I contacted his doctor, but as far as I know no action was taken. But I don't like the way this business is developing, and I'm coming along to the Clinic immediately. I shan't come in, but I'll be around in the grounds, watching for Craig. If he shows up then I'll get him.'

'Thank you, Sergeant. I thought I'd better let you know the situation. Nurse Gerard did say that Craig made some threats against me, and she thought he might have done her some harm if she hadn't humoured him.'

'Very well, Sister! You can safely leave it in my hands now. If I want to see you I'll come into the Clinic, but you can rest assured that I shall be on the spot all night.'

The line went dead and Lydia hung up, sitting for a moment lost in thought. She knew she had done the right thing. She could not afford to take chances! She suppressed a sigh and tried to force her mind to concentrate upon her duties. When she went through the reports on the desk she found that she could hardly see the writing, and she sighed in frustration as she got up from the desk and began her first round. The exercise helped her mind, but by the time she got back to the office she was still in no fit mental state to do her paperwork.

But routine helped her a lot, and she forced herself to keep her mind on what she was doing. Her nerves seemed stretched very tightly, and the thought that Craig might be out there somewhere in the darkness, waiting his chance to get into the Clinic, made her imagination run riot. It gave a sense of unreality to the situation.

When Tim appeared Lydia was most relieved, and she let her expression show her pleasure.

'Do you feel better about coming back now that you're in harness again?' he demanded gently.

'I'm all right now,' she responded with a smile. 'But it was the first time I've ever felt reluctant to return. That's what love has done to me, Lydia Redmond, the dedicated nurse who has never swerved from the tight path of duty.'

'It happens to most people in their lives,' he said with a grin. 'But you're looking worried, Lydia. Is anything else on your mind?'

'Nothing, Tim. It's night duty, I expect. I shall be coming on to days in another week, and then you'll see the difference in me.'

'I can't wait for that to happen. We'll be on a normal footing then. There's nothing more frustrating for a man to have to take his girl home long before a respectable time because she's got to go on night duty.'

Lydia smiled, and she went with him on a round of the patients. She took the opportunity, because he was with her, to check all the empty rooms in the Clinic, and Tim helped her to examine all the outside windows. There was a broken pane in a window of one of the unoccupied rooms, and Lydia knew it was how Craig had forced his way into the Clinic on Friday evening when he had taken hold of Nurse Gerard. The lock on the door seemed loose, and she realized that Craig must have removed it completely from the inside in order to circumvent the lock. Tim exclaimed about the broken window, and Lydia said she would make a report to get it fixed next day.

She was quite happy that Craig had not yet gained access to the interior of the Clinic, and with the police watching in the grounds she felt certain that Craig would be apprehended if he showed his face. The fact that he hadn't called her on the telephone made her think that perhaps he was planning a personal visit, and she was still tense when she returned to her office and Tim went off to get some sleep.

Nurse Gerard went for her meal shortly after, and Lydia kept a watchful eye on both floors of patients. She kept glancing at the telephone, afraid that it would ring, knowing that if it did, Terry Craig would be on the other end. But midnight came and went, and the second stage of her night duty began to unfold.

She wondered if the police were still outside in the grounds as the early hours passed. She could sometimes hear rain beating frenziedly against the windows, and although she felt secure within, she was concerned about those less fortunate, who were waiting around because she had been afraid of what might happen.

Morning came all too slowly for her, and Lydia didn't know if she was relieved or not that the night had brought no terrors. When she was relieved she went to breakfast, and said little to Nurse Gerard, who was filled with garrulous pleasure at having finished her duty.

'Well there was no disturbance during the night,' Nurse Gerard said with a laugh. 'If Craig came at all then he must have seen or sensed the police were waiting for him. But he won't be put off by that. Sister. He's going to bide his time and get to you when he has the opportunity. If I were you I wouldn't leave the Clinic alone again. He's always watching the place.'

'You're certain he said he'd come and see me?' Lydia demanded.

'He said it several times. He was beside himself with impatience to get his hands on you.'

Lydia finished her meal and went up to her room, wandering around and doing all the odd jobs she could find before settling down to sleep, afraid that if she tried to rest too soon her teeming mind would keep her awake. But she fell asleep as soon as her head touched the pillow, and it was past two-thirty when she awoke that afternoon.

As soon as she went down for her meal she was approached by one of the duty nurses with a message that the police sergeant would be coming to see her at three-fifteen. She digested this information more easily than she ate her meal, and she was glad that Nurse Gerard hadn't put in an appearance because she didn't feel up to the sort of chatter she would get from her younger colleague. But when Tim appeared as she was finishing her meal she realized that word of the situation existing at night in the Clinic had gone around through the usual channels.

'Lydia, why didn't you tell me last night why you were so security conscious?' he demanded almost angrily. His blue eyes were very bright, and she could see that he was disturbed by what he had heard.

'I didn't want word of this getting around the staff at large,' she said.

'But surely I have a right to know,' he retorted. 'I wouldn't have gone to bed at all if I had known what sort of trouble we have here.'

'That's why I didn't tell you,' she said with a weary smile.

'Well I'm going to have a word with that detective when he comes this afternoon. This job is demanding enough without you being worried by some lunatic who should be locked up.'

'That's not the way to talk about him, Tim,' she said gently. 'I can understand your anger, but Craig can't help what he's doing. He needs more medical treatment. I showed him some sympathy and he seized upon it.'

'Well if the police can't stop him coming around here than I'm going to have something to say to him myself. Do you know where he lives, Lydia?'

'No, Tim!' She shook her head. 'Look, it isn't as important as you think. Let's forget about it. Now the police know the sort of man he is they'll be able to do something about him.'

'I'm not so sure, and I'm not inclined to take any chances with you! If something happened to you I'd never get over it.'

'Craig isn't that kind of man,' she went on, shaking her head as if trying to convince herself of the truth in her own words. 'I think the last thing he would try and do is hurt me! I'm the only one who has shown him any sympathy, and that's what he needs.'

'I wish you had told me all about him when it first happened,' Tim said softly.

She looked him in the eyes, shaking her head slowly. 'I'm sorry now that I didn't, but it was only because I was afraid you would take it the wrong way, Tim. I was afraid to open the way for any complications.'

'Anything I didn't like about it wouldn't have been half so bad as the experiences you've had since this started,' he retorted. 'Surely you didn't think I'd turn so jealous that I'd think of parting from you!'

'There was that possibility! I just couldn't risk it.'

He smiled his understanding and reached towards her, taking her hands in his and gripping them reassuringly.

'I'd never leave you, my dearest,' he said fervently. 'I love you with all my heart.'

She was relieved by his words, knowing that she had been wrong in not telling him what was happening, but now he knew, and he was not going to let the facts upset him.

'But it doesn't alter matters, Lydia,' he said seriously. 'You're not to leave the Clinic unless you're accompanied by me, you know.' He paused for a moment and studied her, until she could not bear the scrutiny any longer.

'What's the matter?' she demanded.

'That night we parked and someone came up and peered in at the car window! Would that have been this chap Craig?'

'I rather fancy it was.' She nodded. 'He did see us together, and I suspect that he followed us.'

Tim nodded, his face clearing a little. 'Well there's nothing to worry about so long as you don't go out alone. I can't see the police letting him remain at large after this. He's making a real nuisance of himself.'

Lydia agreed. She got up from her seat and they walked to the door.

'Are we going out this evening?' Tim demanded.

'I don't know what to do while this situation holds,' she said. 'We don't know what Terry Craig will do. I'm sure he's getting in such a mental state that he doesn't know right from wrong.'

'If he is as bad as that then he certainly should be put away. I'll be with you when this policeman comes to talk to you, Lydia. I want to know what's being done.'

'I shall feel easier if you are with me,' she retorted.

They parted then, but Tim promised to be on hand, and Lydia went up to her room until it was time to see the policeman. When she returned to the ground floor later she found Tim already in the hall, and the police sergeant was with him.

'I was about to send for you, Lydia,' Tim said. 'But I wanted to have a word with the Sergeant first.' He glanced at the policeman. 'Perhaps you'd better come along to my office,' he suggested.

'Thank you, and I would also like to talk to Nurse Gerard about last Friday night,' Sergeant Swinfield said. 'I have to get a statement from her.'

'Were you outside all last night?' Lydia asked as they walked along to Tim's office.

'I was there until about three-thirty, then someone took over from me, but as I was telling Doctor Fairfax, there was no sign of Craig.'

'He didn't telephone me either,' Lydia said thoughtfully. 'I hope I didn't give you a night's work unnecessarily, Sergeant.'

'I would rather waste a night like that than underestimate the situation and find out too late that there's been some kind of an incident.'

They entered the office and sat down, and Tim departed again to send someone to fetch Nurse Gerard. Lydia watched the sergeant's face as he produced his notebook. She was again seized by a sense of unreality, and she shook her head slowly as she waited for him to get down to business.

'I'm afraid I've been unable to find Craig,' he said suddenly, looking up at her with sharp brown eyes. 'I went to his home this morning and his father told me that he'd gone out yesterday and didn't return. But it seems that he's in a habit of doing things like that so there's no cause for alarm. When I explained the situation to Mr Craig he agreed to take his son to see their doctor as soon as he returns home, and he's going to make sure that Craig doesn't come around here again.'

'Well that's a relief!' Lydia sighed heavily, and felt something like a load lift from her shoulders. 'It is good news, Sergeant. It's been a bit nerve-racking here, wondering if someone was going to spring out of an unoccupied room.'

'We shan't relax our vigilance until we know where he is,' Swinfield said. 'There are two cases of assault that I'm investigating, and truth to tell, I feel that Craig knows something about them. But I can't shake his story yet!'

'It's a dreadful business, especially as he's ill and not responsible for his actions.'

'You believe that, do you?

'I'm certain of it, judging from what I've heard him say, and just by looking at him. He's living under a severe mental strain. Something must be done to help him.'

'He'll get all the help he needs when we find him,' came the firm reply. 'But you will report to us if you hear from him, won't you?'

'Of course!' Lydia nodded.

'That's what I want to talk to you about. If he calls you and asks to meet you then make arrangements to see him, but we shall keep the appointment, of course.'

Lydia looked doubtful, and the Sergeant hastened to reassure her.

'We must find him quickly. You realize that more than anyone. If he is responsible for these other attacks on girls then he must be as badly off mentally as you think, and the next time he stops a girl he might go too far. So if he calls, make an arrangement to see him, then tip us off.'

'I'll do it,' Lydia said, nodding and sighing.

'Thank you, Sister. I do appreciate the spirit in which you have acted, and I sincerely hope we can help Craig when we get to him. This place will be under surveillance until we do pick him up, so don't worry about tonight or any other night.'

'I rather fancy that Doctor Fairfax will be keeping an eye open now he knows about this,' Lydia said. 'I ought to have told him about it before this.'

'Well you can get away now, Sister!' He checked his notebook. 'Just be sympathetic with Craig if he calls you, and don't arouse his suspicions.'

'Do you think he might have seen something suspicious last night, Sergeant?' Lydia demanded.

'He wouldn't have spotted us. We didn't advertise our presence. I had a car drop me off up the road, and I walked the rest of the way, sneaking into the grounds and concealing myself near the building where I could watch approaches. I made several silent patrols around the place, but I didn't see anything suspicious. He wasn't around last night or I would have seen him.'

Lydia nodded, and got up to leave. But Tim returned at that moment and he had Nurse Gerard with him. Lydia smiled reassuringly at the girl and continued on her way out. Tim ushered Nurse Gerard into the office, then followed Lydia.

She told him all that had passed between her and the sergeant, and Tim nodded confidently.

'He's on top of his job,' he said. 'I don't doubt that he knows exactly what he's talking about. No harm will come to you now, Lydia, and they'll soon pick up Craig.'

'I'm not worried now I've managed to convince everyone how serious a matter this is,' she said. 'I'm quite relieved, and I hope they catch him quickly, before he has the chance to make things worse for himself.'

'We'll go out for a drive and a drink this evening,' Tim told her. 'I haven't been too happy today, and not only because of the news about this incident with Craig. I've never known anything like it before, Lydia. I've been walking around the Clinic feeling as if all the troubles in the world were resting upon my shoulders. I've been wishing that we could have the week-end all over again.'

Lydia smiled as she studied his intent face. 'That's how I felt all yesterday,' she said. 'What's your diagnosis of two people feeling that way?'

'I'd say with no hesitation that they must be deeply in love with one another!' His blue eyes were gleaming. 'What do you think, Sister?'

'I agree with you!'

He glanced at his watch. 'We must finish this chat tonight, Lydia. See you at seven!'

'I'll be ready,' she promised.

He departed on his duties and Lydia waited for Nurse Gerard to emerge from the office. When the girl appeared the sergeant was with her, and he left the Clinic quickly, after reassuring them again that the matter was well in hand.

'What did he want to know from you, Nurse?' Lydia asked the girl.

'I had to make a statement about Friday night. I don't want to make any trouble for Craig, but we can't be too careful, can we?'

'That's how I feel about it! It's got beyond a joke, and it could go a lot further without much prompting from anyone. That man is ill, Nurse, and he needs urgent medical treatment.'

'Well I hope they soon catch him. It's bad enough as it is, being on night duty, but when there's someone like Terry Craig prowling around it's enough to send you up the wall. I just can't help expecting him to spring out from some doorway, or walk around a corner and scare the wits out of me.'

'You know that you started this in the first place by teasing him, don't you?' Lydia said quietly.

'I know,' came the contrite reply. 'I shall be more careful in future, don't you worry.'

Lydia nodded. There was nothing else to say.

Later, Tim called for her, and they went out for the evening. Lydia could not help peering around into the shadows as they left the Clinic, fearful that she would see Craig's Mini, but there was no sign of the vehicle, and she breathed a little easier when they reached town without incident.

'You're rather silent, Lydia,' Tim observed. 'Are you still worried about this business?'

'I've got it on my mind,' she confessed. 'I shan't feel easy again until I know the police have found him.'

'Well you've got nothing to worry about while you're with me,' he retorted. 'I fancy that I can take care of you, no matter what happens.'

Lydia agreed, but she could not set her mind at ease. The evening passed all too quickly, and when they parked just before returning to the Clinic, she was most uneasy, glancing around every few moments, until Tim sighed and shook his head.

'I think we'd better get back to the Clinic,' he said. 'You're on tenterhooks, Lydia, and it isn't doing your nerves any good. You keep looking outside. Are you expecting this man to come up to the car?'

'Well we thought he did the other evening, didn't we?' she countered.

'You're right.' He sighed again. 'Come on, let's go home. We'll have to take it easy until this business is settled one way or another.'

She was thoughtful on the drive back to the Clinic, although she looked fearfully at every car which passed them. But she saw nothing of Craig's car, and she only wondered all the more about him. Where had he disappeared to? What state was his mind in now? What could have happened to him?

They reached the Clinic without incident, but she was not happy. When they went into the building, Tim kissed her goodnight and went off, while she went to her room to prepare for duty. As soon as she entered the room and switched on the light she sensed something was wrong, and as she turned away from the door to look swiftly around the room, her heart missed a beat in shock, for Craig himself was sitting on the bed.

Gasping, Lydia fell back a step, but she had no thought for flight. Then she saw that Craig had something in his hands, and horror swamped through her when she recognized the article as a shotgun!

Chapter Thirteen

'I've been waiting for you to come back,' Craig said heavily, and he did not stir from the foot of the bed where he was sitting. The gun in his hands was immobile, and its shiny barrel fascinated Lydia. The fact that he did not move it made her feel all the more terrified. His eyes were gleaming, and he seemed to be waiting for her to do something foolish, as if he were a large cat of prey awaiting the first signs of fear in its victim before pouncing.

Lydia made a supreme effort to remain calm, and she breathed deeply as she tried to contain the panic that threatened to engulf her.

'Where have you been in the past few days?' she demanded, striving to make her tones normal. 'I've been worried about you, fearing that you were taken ill somewhere and couldn't get help.'

'You've been worried about me?' Surprise touched his tones and he frowned.

'Of course! You know I've been worried about you for some time. I kept trying to get you to see your doctor again before last week-end.'

'You've made a lot of trouble for me,' he said thickly, taking a deep breath.

'I've been trying to help you,' she countered. 'What are you doing here now? I told you after the last time that it just isn't the thing to do. Why don't you act as if you were responsible?'

'I know the police are watching this place. It gives me a kick to outwit them. I've been sitting in here laughing to myself because they're out there in the night, hoping to set eyes on my sneaking figure.'

'How do you know the police are watching the Clinic?'

'My father told me when I went home earlier this evening.'

'Where have you been since Friday night?'

'I was here on Friday night. I wanted so badly to talk to you.'

'I told you over the phone before Friday that I wouldn't be here over the week-end.'

'I forgot about it until I arrived. But Nurse Gerard is all right. She promised to help me.'

'In what way?' Lydia sensed that she had to humour him, give him no cause for alarm or anger, but how she was going to get out of this she just didn't know. She didn't like the fact that he had brought a gun along, and a shiver spread through her as she imagined that he was even now contemplating using it.

'She's going to try and cause a split between you and that Doctor Fairfax.'

'Why should she want to do that? Is she interested in Doctor Fairfax.'

'No, but I'm interested in you. If Fairfax wasn't on the scene then I'd have a chance with you. I can sense that, you do like me, don't you?'

'How could I lie to you, seeing that gun in your hands?' she demanded boldly. 'Why have you brought that gun along tonight, Terry? Don't you know you could scare someone half to death, just having it along?'

'That was the intention when I first came!'

'To scare me?' Lydia was breathing heavily through her mouth, conscious of the fact that she could not afford to make a mistake of judgement. There was a brightness in his eyes that warned her he could be most unstable. But she imagined she was using the right tone of voice and the correct manner in handling him. She knew her life depended upon her being correct, and that knowledge did nothing for her peace of mind. She moved to a seat and dropped lightly into it, leaning forward and studying his face as if they were old friends.

'Why should I want to scare you?' he demanded. 'I'm in love with you.'

'Do you always take a shotgun along when you visit someone you like?' she asked.

'Of course not. I brought it along because

I want to throw a scare into that doctor friend of yours if I see him. Why don't you get him to come on up here so I can let him see the kind of person I really am?'

'I don't think that would be a good idea, Terry. Doctor Fairfax is busy with his patients right now.'

'He's off duty tonight! I saw the two of you going out earlier.'

'Where were you when you saw us?'

'That would be telling. But we're going to get out of here now! I want you to go with me now!'

'But I've got to go on duty now!' Lydia suppressed a sigh. 'Look, you'll only make trouble for yourself if you try to do anything foolish. Let me go on duty and I'll try and see you later. We can talk this over, can't we?'

'You weren't prepared to talk it over earlier. Now you're scared because I've brought this gun along. That's why I brought it. I knew it would make you take me seriously. I can tell by your face that you're scared.'

'I'm only scared for you. If you really want to see me – if you are interested in me, then this isn't the way you should show it. Act properly and I'll talk it over with you.'

'You're just playing for time. The minute I put this gun down you'll ring the police.'

'Certainly not. I've been bending over backwards trying to get you out of trouble. I've persuaded everyone here, and the police, that you were only playing a joke on me when you came here before. That's why the police haven't preferred charges against you. Can't you see that coming with that gun tonight proves that it's no longer a joke? If you're seen leaving with it then you'll be in very serious trouble.'

'Anyone who sees me leaving will be in worse trouble,' he retorted furiously.

She could see his manner changing quickly, and hopelessness flared inside her. He was getting out of hand, and nothing she said would have any effect upon him.

'Look, I must go on duty,' she said again.

'Why don't you put that gun in my cupboard and leave it there? Then you could leave, and if anyone does see you leaving I'll tell the police that you came here to see me with my permission. I would get into trouble if that happened, but it wouldn't matter so much as the trouble you'd find yourself in.'

'That gun stays with me!' he said firmly.

'Then let me lock you in this room while I go on duty, and later, when it's much quieter, I'll get you out of the place without you being seen.'

'I don't care about being seen. This gun will keep everyone away from me. I've had plenty of time to think things over this week-end. I haven't got anything to live for. I might just as well be dead. I can't find peace of mind. The only peace I'll get will come to me when I blow my brains out!'

'That kind of talk will do no one any good,' she said firmly. She was beginning to feel panic welling up inside her. If she didn't put in an appearance at the dining room soon then Nurse Gerard at least would be coming up to the room to find out where she was. It might be the distraction that would start him off into the realms of instability. She could see he was wavering now between the disenchanting fact of having to do what she said and the dictates of his anguished mind. He wanted to hurt someone because he had been badly hurt in the past.

'You come with me and I'll go,' he said. 'I've got a strange compulsion inside me. I want to do something evil, terrible, and I have to start with you. I can hear a voice in my mind telling me that the only way I'll find peace is by doing this.'

'I wish you would listen to me and be guided by me,' Lydia said slowly. 'You're attracted to me, Terry, aren't you?'

'I have been from the start.'

'Then why not take advantage of the fact that I'm prepared to see you, do anything to help you? If you do something terrible then all your chances will be gone. You'll be wasting everything you ever had.'

'I can't trust you now. You're just talking like this because you're afraid of what I might do. If you had treated me like this only a few days ago I would have believed you, but now I know you are just trying to humour me.'

'Think of your father!' she said desperately, and saw a harsh expression come to his face. His eyes were wide and filled with coldness, and Lydia felt her heart quail as she realized that she was not having the desired effect upon him.

'My father wishes I'd never been born! He never wanted me. I know for a fact that he doesn't care what happens to me.'

'I'm sure that's not true. Look, I'll come home with you if you like, and talk to your father. You need more medical attention, Terry, and then you'll be perfectly all right. You'll think quite differently after you've had more treatment.'

'I'm not interested in that any more. I had enough of it the last time I was in hospital.'

'Look, I do have to go on duty! Won't you stay hidden here until I've reported and taken care of the more urgent routine? I can come back here later to talk to you.'

'I don't trust you. The first thing you would do if I let you go now is ring the police.'

'I wouldn't do that, Terry! I wouldn't want anyone to get hurt. I know I can talk you round to my way of thinking. You say you're attracted to me! Well do as I say and prove it.'

'I would if that Doctor Fairfax didn't mean anything to you. But you're his girl now.'

Lydia began to have visions of not seeing Tim ever again. She tried hard to suppress her fear, and was careful not to let her manner or her expression show any sign of it.

'What is it you want me to do then?' she demanded.

'Leave here with me or something bad will happen to the rest of the nurses.'

'But I'm due on duty in a very short time.'

'Tell them you're not well enough to go on duty.'

'That will mean a visit from the doctor on duty. He'll have to come into this room. If it is Doctor Fairfax then you might do something foolish, and in any case, he would see you here.'

'Then you won't go with me?'

'Not while you've got that gun. I would rather you shot me here and now and fled without doing harm to anyone else than go with you knowing that you would shoot the first person, and every person who got in your way.'

He stood up slowly and confronted her, and Lydia felt a coldness seeping into her heart as she watched him lift the gun and level it at her. She looked into the gaping muzzle of the weapon and almost fainted in fright, but she fought her fears and remained outwardly calm.

'I can't believe you would harm someone who has only your best interests at heart,' she said in wavering tones. 'I understand that some of the girls have made fun of you, Terry. You got the idea of coming here in the first place from a joke Nurse Gerard was playing on you. But I've never felt anything but sympathy for you. I want to help you. A man doesn't hurt his friends, Terry.'

She saw an expression of pure agony touch his face, and he shook his head slowly. But she didn't know what else to say. Her nerve was letting her down now. She could feel an awful trembling inside, and it was increasing and beating down her determination.

'I don't want to hurt you,' he said. 'It's those others I ought to do for.'

'Let's talk some more about your problems,' she said. 'Your mother is dead, you told me once. Tell me some more about her. Think of her, Terry, and tell me if she would be pleased that you are here tonight with those intentions you have in mind.'

'I don't want to talk about her. She's dead and gone, and no amount of talking will ever bring her back.'

'She still lives in you! She brought you into the world. You are her flesh and blood. Have you ever stopped to consider that?'

Before he could answer there was the sound of footsteps in the corridor, and Lydia tensed and moved back to the door, afraid that someone was coming to her room. Her eyes were upon Craig's harsh face, and she saw desperation come into his eyes.

'If it's anyone for you, don't let them in,' he warned, brandishing the gun. 'Tell them you're not well enough to go on duty.'

Before Lydia could argue with him there was a tap at the door, and she felt a deadly paralysis seeping into her mind. The knowledge that she might do the wrong thing and trigger this man into fatal action was devastating her mind, and she had to make a supreme effort to hang on to her control. The knocking was repeated, louder this time, and she tried to moisten her lips.

'Tell them what I said,' Craig hissed.

Lydia gulped at the lump in her throat. When she tried to speak she found her voice non-existent, but she forced herself into speech.

'Who's there?' she demanded in high, unnatural tones.

'Nurse Gerard, Sister. You haven't been down to the dining room yet, and it's almost time for you to go on duty. Are you all right? Are you ready for duty?'

'I'm sorry but I can't make it tonight, Nurse. I've got the most dreadful headache, and I can't even lift my head from the pillow. Will you see to it that someone goes on in my place? You can tell Doctor Fairfax that it's my old trouble! He gave me some pills for it last week, but they haven't done any good. I told him earlier that I wasn't feeling well.'

'Can I get you something, Sister?'

'No thank you. You can't get into the room. I bolted the door before I lay down, and I don't feel up to getting to my feet to unbolt it. Just leave me and I shall be all right by morning.'

'All right if you say so, but I think the doctor ought to see you!'

'Forget about me. Just tell Doctor Fairfax that it's my old trouble and he'll know it's nothing to worry about.'

Lydia waited then with bated breath, and she was relieved when she heard the girl's footsteps receding. She sighed heavily, and yet she was still dreadfully worried. If Nurse Gerard gave Tim the message then he would know something was wrong because he hadn't given her any pills for headache. But would he use his sense and contact the police with his suspicions, or would he come up here and try to get into the room to her?

'Was that all right?' she asked Craig, who was watching her intently.

'You've done the right thing,' he said grudgingly. 'Although I think I ought to have got Nurse Gerard in here. I owe her something for the way she's mocked me in the past.'

'Forget about her! Put her actions down to

her ignorance.' Lydia felt the need to impress him with her friendliness, and she moved towards him, but the muzzle of the gun lifted and stopped her again.

'We're getting out of here now,' he warned. 'If they come up here to check on you then I'll shoot someone, I promise you. We're going out the window and down the fire escape, and if you make any noise or attract anyone's attention there will be bloodshed.'

'I'll go with you,' she said without hesitation. 'You don't need that gun where I'm concerned, Terry. Come on, before anyone does come up here to check.'

She crossed instantly to the window and opened it, and started climbing over the sill to the fire escape before he was ready. He came close behind her and grasped her arm, holding her tightly for a moment, and his eyes seemed to blaze with inner fires.

'Remember what I said about making a noise,' he said. 'There is a policeman on watch in the grounds, and I'll kill him if he becomes aware of our presence.'

'Don't keep that gun pointed at me,' she pleaded. 'If you slip it will go off and kill me. I'm not going to do anything against you. I'll go with you willingly enough, if only to get you away from here.'

He nodded, and she continued out through the window, pausing on the wet fire escape, waiting for him to join her. He followed her quickly and slid down the window.

'That way,' he said sharply, and took her elbow, pushing her in the direction he wished to go. They reached the corner of the building and descended the flight of steps to the ground. He held her in the deeper shadows for a moment, looking around, listening intently, and Lydia could not help thinking that this was all part of some dreadful nightmare. She was breathing heavily, and fear lay like an intolerable burden in her mind, but she was relieved that they were leaving the Clinic. At least no other innocent life was now in danger. She didn't really care what happened now that particular threat had been removed.

Craig led her through the bushes, proving that he had an intimate knowledge of the grounds, and she could not help wondering how many times he had skulked around here in the past, unknown to anyone. He might have been playing Peeping Tom for months!

When they reached the perimeter wall they walked through the shadows until they came to a small door. To Lydia's surprise Craig produced a key and unlocked the door, and he chuckled harshly as they passed through and went outside.

'I had a key made,' he said as he took her arm and hurried her along the muddy lane. 'Come on, my car's down here.'

'We're going for a drive?' she demanded tensely.

'I'm taking you away from here,' he retorted. 'That's all you need to know right now.'

Lydia had no choice but to go along with

him, and she thought of Tim and the rest of the staff as they went further from the Clinic. What would Tim do? Would he be able to suspect something was wrong from the message she had given Nurse Gerard?

Her hopes and fears were inextricably mixed as she stumbled the uncertain path to Craig's car. When they reached the vehicle he paused and stood chuckling in triumph. Lydia felt her flesh crawl at the note of hysteria she detected in his tones, and she glanced around quickly, wondering if she could chance a run for it into the night. But the knowledge that the shotgun would blast her if she tried anything stole the strength from her legs, and she was trembling and afraid as she awaited his next action.

He unlocked the car door and stepped aside for her to get in. She did so, and he slammed the door on her, hurrying around the small car to get behind the wheel. Lydia was watching him closely, praying for any sort of a chance to aid her in escape, and her heart fluttered with anticipation when she saw him put the gun into the back of the car before getting into the driving seat. In the instant that he slid behind the wheel she thrust open her door and hurled herself recklessly from the vehicle, falling heavily upon the muddy road and rolling lithely to come to her feet. Then she started running blindly, aware that he was cursing and fighting his surprise to come in pursuit.

Lydia was mindful of the gun, and she knew he lost valuable seconds in pursuit by pausing to snatch the gun from the back of the car. When she judged that he had got the gun in his hands she turned aside and leaped into the ditch at the side of the road, thankful that she knew this area very well. She fell into the icy water, and lay there, partly submerged, her shoulders heaving, her breath searing her throat as she panted.

She knew she couldn't outrun him, and the gun was a factor that outweighed all other considerations. She crouched in the dark water and waited, hearing Craig's running footsteps and his furious cursing rage. He went by her position, intent upon catching her, and she felt a small measure of relief seep into her mind as he continued to run as fast as he could along the road.

Knowing that he would come back as soon as he realized that she had dodged him, Lydia got to her feet and slithered out of the ditch. She started back as fast as she could go towards the door in the wall, knowing there would be a policeman on duty somewhere in the grounds. Her breath was catching in her throat by the time she reached the door, and she paused for a moment to turn and peer in the direction that Craig had taken.

At that moment a pair of hands came out of the doorway and took hold of her, and Lydia felt her heart miss a beat in sudden fear. But the hands were gentle and comforting, and she gasped her relief as she threw herself into Tim's arms.

'You're all right now, darling,' he said softly. 'Come along inside and leave Craig to the police.'

Lydia saw figures lurking in the shadows, and her fear began to recede, but shock still gripped her, and she swayed and clung to Tim as if she couldn't believe it was really he.

But Tim ushered her through the gateway, and Lydia saw the policemen closing in about the aperture. Someone whispered a sibilant warning, and Tim hurried Lydia away from the door, pushing her behind a tree and holding her tightly.

Lydia insisted upon looking at the doorway, and she saw movement there as Craig returned. For an instant she saw him standing in the doorway, the long gun in his hands, and then there was an ejaculation and a sudden scramble, and she saw Craig going down on the ground with several policemen attacking him. She averted her eyes and pressed her face against Tim's thick shoulder.

'The police found Craig's car outside while he was in your room, dearest,' Tim said gently. 'Nurse Gerard came for you on their instigation, and your reply to her told them what they wanted to know, that Craig was in there with you. You were under surveillance from the moment he forced you on to the fire escape, but because of the gun they dared not close in. His car wouldn't have started even if you hadn't made that dash for it when you did. It had been immobilized. He would have been jumped the moment he put down the gun to seek out the trouble.'

'Oh, Tim!' She could feel relief flushing up in her breast, and a figure was coming towards them from the doorway. 'Tim, it was like a nightmare.'

'But it's all over now,' Tim responded. 'Is he under control now, Sergeant?'

'He's been handcuffed, Doctor,' came the steady reply. 'I thought you'd like to know, Sister, that he's protesting that he meant you no harm. But we'll go into that later, shall we?'

'I'm sure he wouldn't have hurt me.' Lydia suppressed a shiver. The keen night wind was blowing right through her soaked clothes. 'But I've got to get on duty. You'll know where to find me, Sergeant, if you need a statement.'

'I shall certainly need one, Sister,' came the reply.

Tim started leading her towards the building, and Lydia let her weight rest upon his hand. She was suddenly filled with an overwhelming sense of relief, and she turned to Tim and pulled him to a halt.

'What's the matter?' he demanded.

'Nothing now,' she retorted. 'I just want you to kiss me.'

He obliged quickly, and when she would have dallied longer he took her arm and began to hurry her towards the Clinic.

'Do you want to catch pneumonia?' he demanded. 'You're soaked to the skin. We've got all our lives before us to kiss and make plans.'

'All our lives,' she repeated, and flung herself into his arms again. 'Tell me you love me, Tim!'

'I love you, Lydia, more than anything in the world!'

'A short time ago I thought I'd never hear you say that again,' she whispered. 'But now you must make me a promise.'

'Anything,' he said eagerly.

'Tell me that you love me every single day in future.'

'I shan't need any prompting!' He gathered her close once more and kissed her.

Lydia closed her eyes, unmindful of her soaked clothes and the biting wind. She was warm inside where her love rested, and Tim kissed her, and went on kissing her, and suddenly it didn't matter about words, or the past. The future was all that counted, and it was there before them like a beckoning road impatient for their feet. Lydia knew then it was good to be alive, and with her work and her love she would be forever thankful that her lot was happy. Above all, she and Tim had each other!

The publishers hope that this book has given you enjoyable reading. Large Print Books are especially designed to be as easy to see and hold as possible. If you wish a complete list of our books please ask at your local library or write directly to:

Dales Large Print Books
Magna House, Long Preston,
Skipton, North Yorkshire.
BD23 4ND

This Large Print Book for the partially sighted, who cannot read normal print, is published under the auspices of
THE ULVERSCROFT FOUNDATION